The Carpet People

TERRY PRATCHETT

THE CARPET PEOPLE

DOUBLEDAY

LONDON . NEW YORK . TORONTO . SYDNEY . AUCKLAND

TRANSWORLD PUBLISHERS LTD
61–63 Uxbridge Road, London W5 5SA

TRANSWORLD PUBLISHERS (AUSTRALIA) PTY LTD
15–23 Helles Avenue, Moorebank, NSW 2170

TRANSWORLD PUBLISHERS (NZ) LTD
3 William Pickering Drive,
Albany, Auckland

DOUBLEDAY CANADA LTD
105 Bond Street, Toronto, Ontario M5B 1Y3

First published in 1971 by Colin Smythe Ltd

Revised edition published 1992 by Doubleday
a division of Transworld Publishers Ltd

A catalogue record for this book is available
from the British Library

ISBN 0 385 403046

Typeset by Falcon Typographic Art Ltd, Edinburgh
Printed in Great Britain
by Mackays of Chatham Plc, Chatham, Kent

To Lyn, for then and now.

Author's Note

This book had two authors, and they were both the same person.

The Carpet People was published in 1971. It had a lot of things wrong with it, mostly to do with being written by someone who was seventeen at the time.

And it sold a bit, and eventually it sold out. And that was it.

And then about seven years ago the Discworld books began to sell, and people would buy them and say, 'Here, what's this book *The Carpet People* by The Same Author?' and the publishers got so fed up with telling people that there was no demand for it that they decided it was time for a new edition.

Which was read by Terry Pratchett, aged forty-three, who said: hang on. I wrote that in the days when I thought fantasy was all battles and kings. Now I'm inclined to think that the *real* concerns of fantasy ought to be about not having battles, and doing *without* kings. I'll just rewrite it here and there . . .

Well, you know how it is when you tweak a thread that's hanging loose . . .

So this is it. It's not exactly the book I wrote then. It's not exactly the book I'd write now. It's a joint effort but, heh heh, I don't have to give him half the royalties. He'd only waste them.

You asked for it. Here it is. Thanks.

Incidentally, the size of the city of Ware is approximately →.

Terry Pratchett
September 15, 1991

Prologue

They called themselves the Munrungs. It meant The People, or The True Human Beings.

It's what most people call themselves, to begin with. And then one day the tribe meets some other people, and gives them a name like The Other People or, if it's not been a good day, The Enemy. If only they'd think up a name like Some More True Human Beings, it'd save a lot of trouble later on.

Not that the Munrungs were in any way primitive. Pismire said they had a rich native cultural inheritance. He meant stories.

Pismire knew all the old stories and many new ones and used to tell them while the whole tribe listened, enthralled, and the night-time fires crumbled to ashes.

Sometimes it seemed that even the mighty hairs that grew outside the village stockade listened, too. They seemed to crowd in closer.

The oldest story was the shortest. He did not tell it often, but the tribe knew it by heart. It was a story told in many languages, all over the Carpet.

'In the beginning,' said Pismire, 'there was nothing but endless flatness. Then came the Carpet, which covered the flatness. It was young in those days. There was no dust among the hairs. They were slim and straight, not bent and crusty like they are today. And the Carpet was empty.

'Then came the dust, which fell upon the Carpet, drifting among the hairs, taking root in the deep shadows. More came, tumbling slowly and with silence among the waiting hairs, until the dust was thick in the Carpet.

'From the dust the Carpet wove us all. First came the little crawling creatures that make their dwellings in burrows and high in the hairs. Then came the soraths, and the weft borers, tromps, goats, gromepipers and the snargs.

'Now the Carpet had life and noise. Yes, and death and silence. But there was a thread missing from the weave on the loom of life.

'The Carpet was full of life, but it did not know it was alive. It could *be*, but it could not *think*. It did not even know what it was.

'And so from the dust came us, the Carpet People. We gave the Carpet its name, and named the creatures, and the weaving was complete. We were the first to give the Carpet a name. Now it knew about itself.

'Though Fray, who hates life in the Carpet, may tread upon us, though shadows grow over us, we are the soul of the Carpet, and that is a mighty thing. We are the fruit of the loom.

'Of course, this is all metaphorical but I think it's important, don't you?'

Chapter 1

It was the Law that, every tenth year, the people of all the tribes in the Dumii Empire should come and be Counted.

They did not go all the way to the great capital city of Ware, but to the little walled town of Tregon Marus.

The Counting was always a great occasion. Tregon Marus would double in size and importance overnight as tribal tents were pitched outside its walls. There was a horse market, and a five-day fair, old friends to be met, and a flood of news to be exchanged.

And there was the Counting itself. New names were added to the crackling scrolls which, the people liked to believe, were taken to Ware, even to the Great Palace of the Emperor himself. The Dumii clerks laboriously wrote down how many pigs and goats and tromps everybody had, and one by one the people shuffled on to the next table and paid their taxes in furs and skins. That was the unpopular part. So the queue wound round Tregon Marus, in at the East Gate, through the postern and stables, across the market square, and through the countinghouse. Even the youngest babies were carried past the clerks, for the quill pens to wobble and scratch their names on the parchment. Many a tribesman got a funny name because a clerk didn't know how to spell, and there's more of that sort of thing in History than you might expect.

On the fifth day the Governor of the town called all the tribal chieftains to an audience in the market square, to hear their grievances. He didn't always do anything about them, but at least they got *heard*, and he nodded a lot, and everyone felt better about it at least until they got home. This is politics.

That was how it had always happened, time out of mind.

And on the sixth day the people went back to their homes, along the roads the Dumii had built. They went east. Behind them the road went west, until it came to the city of Ware. There it was just one of the many roads that entered the city. Beyond Ware it became the West Road, becoming narrower and more winding until it reached the furthermost western outpost of Rug.

Such was the Dumii Empire. It covered almost all of the Carpet from the Woodwall to the wasteland near Varnisholme in the north.

In the west it bordered Wildland and the uttermost fringes of the Carpet, and southwards the roads ran as far as the Hearthlands. The painted people of the Wainscot, the warlike Hibbolgs, even the fire-worshippers of Rug, all paid their tribute to the Emperor.

Some of them didn't like the Dumii much, usually because the Empire discouraged the small wars and cattle raids which, in the outlying regions, were by way of being a recreational activity. The Empire liked peace. It meant that people had enough time to earn money to pay their taxes. On the whole, peace seemed to work.

So the Munrung tribe went east, and passed out of the chronicles of the Empire for another ten years. Sometimes they quarrelled among themselves, but on the whole they lived peacefully and avoided having much to do with history, which tends to get people killed.

Then, one year, no more was heard from Tregon Marus . . .

*   *   *

12

Old Grimm Orkson, chieftain of the Munrungs, had two sons. The eldest, Glurk, succeeded his father as chieftain when old Orkson died.

To the Munrung way of thinking, which was a slow and deliberate way, there couldn't have been a better choice. He looked just like a second edition of his father, from his broad shoulders to his great thick neck, the battering centre of his strength. Glurk could throw a spear further than anyone. He could wrestle with a snarg, and wore a necklace of their long yellow teeth to prove it. He could lift a horse with one hand, run all day without tiring, and creep up so close to a grazing animal that sometimes they'd die of shock before he had time to raise his spear. Admittedly he moved his lips when he was thinking, and the thoughts could be seen bumping against one another like dumplings in a stew, but he was not stupid. Not what you'd call stupid. His brain got there in the end. It just went the long way around.

'He's a man of few words, and he doesn't know what either of them mean,' people said, but not when he was within hearing.

One day towards evening he was tramping homeward through the dusty glades, carrying a bone-tipped hunting spear under one arm. The other arm steadied the long pole that rested on his shoulder.

In the middle of the pole, its legs tied together, dangled a snarg. At the other end of the pole was Snibril, Glurk's younger brother.

Old Orkson had married early and lived long, so a wide gap filled by a string of daughters, that the chieftain had carefully married off to upright and respected and above all *well-off* Munrungs, separated the brothers.

Snibril was slight, especially compared with his brother. Grimm had sent him off to the strict Dumii school in Tregon Marus to become a clerk. 'He can't hardly hold a spear,' he said, 'maybe a pen'd be better. Get some learning in the family.'

When Snibril had run away for the third time Pismire came to see Grimm.

Pismire was the shaman, a kind of odd-job priest.

Most tribes had one, although Pismire was different. For one thing, he washed all the bits that showed at least once every month. This was unusual. Other shamen tended to encourage dirt, taking the view that the grubbier, the more magical.

And he didn't wear lots of feathers and bones, and he didn't talk like the other shamen in neighbouring tribes.

Other shamen ate the yellow-spotted mushrooms that were found deep in the hair thickets and said things like: 'Hiiii*yahyah*heya! Heyahey*ayahyah*! *Hngh! Hngh!*' which certainly *sounded* magical.

Pismire said things like, 'Correct observation followed by meticulous deduction and the precise visualization of goals is vital to the success of any enterprise. Have you noticed the way the wild tromps always move around two days ahead of the sorath herds? Incidentally, don't eat the yellow-spotted mushrooms.'

Which didn't sound magical at all, but worked a lot better and conjured up good hunting. Privately some Munrungs thought good hunting was more due to their own skill. Pismire encouraged this view. 'Positive thinking,' he would say, 'is also very important.'

He was also the official medicine man. He was a lot better, they agreed (but reluctantly, because the Munrungs respected tradition) than the last one they had had, whose idea of medicine was to throw some bones in the air and cry 'Hyahyahyah! Hgn! Hgn!' Pismire just mixed various kinds of rare dust in a bowl, made it into pills, and said things like 'Take one of these when you go to bed at night and another one if you wake up in the morning.'

And occasionally he offered advice on other matters.

Grimm was chopping sticks outside his hut. 'It'll never work,' said Pismire, appearing behind him in that silent way of his. 'You can't send Snibril off to Tregon again. He's a Munrung. No wonder he keeps running away. He'll never be a clerk. It's not in the blood, man. Let him stay. I'll see he learns to read.'

'If you can learn him, you're welcome,' said Grimm, shaking his head. 'He's a mystery to me. Spends all his time moping around. His mother used to be like that. Of course, she got a bit of sense once she got married.'

Grimm had never learned to read, but he had always been impressed by the clerks at Tregon Marus. They could make marks on bits of parchment that could *remember* things. That was power, of a sort. He was quite keen to see that an Orkson got some of it.

So Snibril went to Pismire's village school with the other children, and learnt numbers, letters, and the Dumii laws. He enjoyed it, sucking in knowledge as though his life depended on it. It often did, Pismire said.

And, strangely, he also grew up to be a hunter almost as good as his brother. But in different ways. Glurk chased. Snibril *watched*. You don't have to chase around after creatures, Pismire had said. You watch them for long enough, and then you'll find the place to wait and they'll come to *you*. There's nearly always a better way of doing something.

When old Grimm died he was laid in a barrow dug out of the dust of the Carpet, with his hunting spear by his side. Munrungs had no idea where you went when you died, but there was no reason to go hungry once you got there.

Glurk became chieftain, and would have to take the tribe to the next Counting. But the messenger to summon them to Tregon Marus was long overdue, and that worried Glurk. Not that he was in a hurry to pay taxes, and actually going to *see* why the messenger was late seemed a bit too, you know, *keen*, but usually the Dumii were very reliable, especially over tax-gathering.

But as he and his brother wandered homeward that evening he kept his thoughts to himself. Snibril grunted, and heaved the pole on to his other shoulder. He was shorter than his brother, and he was going to get shorter still, he thought, if he couldn't shed the load for a minute or two.

'I feel as though my feet have worn right off and my legs have turned up at the ends,' he said. 'Can't we stop for a rest? Five minutes won't hurt. And . . . my head aches . . .'

'Five minutes, then,' said Glurk. 'No more. It's getting dark.'

They had reached the Dumii road, and not far north of it lay the Woodwall, home and supper. They sat down.

Glurk, who never wasted his time, started to sharpen the point of his spear on a piece of grit, but both brothers gazed down the road, shining in the dim evening air. The road stretched west, a glowing line in the darkness. The hairs around it were full of growing shadows. It had fascinated Snibril, ever since his father had told him that all roads led to Ware. So it was only the road that lay between the doorway of his hut and the threshold of the Emperor's palace, he thought. And if you counted all the streets and passages that led off the road . . . Once you set foot on it you might end up anywhere and if you just sat by the road and waited, who might pass you by? Everywhere was connected to everywhere else, Pismire had said.

He put his head in his hands. The ache was worse. It felt as though he was being squeezed.

The Carpet had felt wrong too, today. The hunting had been hard. Most of the animals had vanished, and the dust between the hairs did not stir in the breathless air.

Glurk said, 'I don't like this. There hasn't been anyone on the road for days.'

He stood up and reached out for the pole.

Snibril groaned. He'd have to ask Pismire for a pill . . .

A shadow flickered high up in the hairs, and flashed away towards the south.

There was a sound so loud as to be felt by the whole body, hitting the Carpet with horrible suddenness. The brothers sprawled in the dust as the hairs around them groaned and screamed in the gale.

Glurk gripped the rough bark of a hair and hauled himself upright, straining against the storm that whipped round him. Far overhead the tip of the hair creaked and rattled, and all round the hairs waved like a grey sea. Smashing through them came grit, man-sized boulders half rolling and half flying before the wind.

Holding on tightly with one hand, Glurk reached out with the other and hauled his brother to safety. Then they crouched, too shaken to speak, while the storm banged about them.

As quickly as it had come, it veered south, and the darkness followed it.

The silence clanged like gongs.

Snibril blinked. Whatever it was, it had taken the headache with it. His ears popped.

Then he heard the sound of hooves on the road as the wind died away.

They got louder very quickly and sounded wild and frightened, as though the horse was running free.

When it appeared, it was riderless. Its ears lay back flat on its head and its eyes flashed green with terror. The white coat glistened with sweat, reins cracked across the saddle with the fury of the gallop.

Snibril leapt in its path. Then, as the creature hurtled by him, he snatched at the reins, raced for a second by the pounding hooves, and flung himself up into the saddle.

Why he dared that he never knew. Careful observation and precise determination of goals, probably. He just couldn't imagine *not* doing it.

They rode into the village, the quietened horse carrying them and dragging the snarg behind it.

The village stockade had broken in several places, and grit boulders had smashed some huts. Glurk looked towards the Orkson hut and Snibril heard the moan that escaped from him. The chieftain climbed down from the horse's back and walked slowly towards his home.

Or what had *been* his home.

The rest of the tribe stopped talking and drew back, awed, to let him pass. A hair had fallen, a big one. It had crushed the stockade. And the tip of it lay across what was left of the Orkson hut, the arch of the doorway still standing bravely amid a litter of beams and thatch. Bertha Orkson came running forward with her children round her, and flung herself into his arms.

'Pismire got us out before the hair fell,' she cried. 'Whatever shall we do?'

He patted her absently but went on staring at the ruined hut. Then he climbed along up the mound of wreckage, and prodded about.

So silent was the crowd that every sound he made echoed. There was a clink as he picked up the pot that had miraculously escaped destruction, and looked at it as though he had never seen its design before, turning it this way and that in the firelight. He raised it above his head and smashed it on the ground.

Then he raised his fist above him and swore. He cursed by the hairs, by the dark caverns of Underlay, by the demons of the Floor, by the Weft and by the Warp. He bellowed the Unutterable Words and swore the oath of Retwatshud the Frugal, that cracked bone, or so it was said, although Pismire claimed that this was superstition.

Curses circled up in the evening hairs and the night creatures of the Carpet listened. Oath was laid upon oath in a towering pillar vibrating terror.

When he had finished the air trembled. He flopped down on the wreckage and sat with his head in his hands, and no-one dared approach. There were sidelong glances, and one or two people shook themselves and hurried away.

Snibril dismounted and wandered over to where Pismire was standing gloomily wrapped in his goatskin cloak.

'He shouldn't have said the Unutterable Words,' said Pismire, more or less to himself, 'It's all superstition, of course, but that's not to say it isn't *real*. Oh, hello. I see you survived.'

'What did this?'

'It used to be called Fray,' said Pismire.

'I thought that was just an old story.'

'Doesn't mean it was untrue. I'm sure it was Fray. The changes in air pressure to begin with . . . the animals sensed it . . . just like it said in the . . .' He stopped. 'Just like I read somewhere,' he said awkwardly.

He glanced past Snibril and brightened up.

'You've got a horse, I see.'

'I think it's been hurt.'

Pismire walked to the horse and examined it carefully. 'It's Dumii, of course,' he said. 'Someone fetch my herb box. Something's attacked him, see, here. Not deep but it should be dressed. A magnificent beast. Magnificent. No rider?'

'We rode up the road a way but we didn't see any-one.'

Pismire stroked the sleek coat. 'If you sold all the village and its people into slavery you might just be able to buy a horse like this. Whoever he belonged to, he ran away some time ago. He's been living wild for days.'

19

'The Dumii don't let anyone keep slaves any more,' said Snibril.

'It's worth a lot is what I was trying to say,' said Pismire.

He hummed distractedly to himself as he examined the hooves.

'Wherever he came from, someone must have been riding him.'

He let one leg go and paused to stare up at the hairs. 'Something scared him. Not Fray. Something days ago. It wasn't bandits, because they would have taken the horse too. And they don't leave claw marks. A snarg could have made that if it was three times its normal size. Oh, dear. And there are such,' he said.

The cry came.

To Snibril it seemed as though the night had grown a mouth and a voice. It came from the hairs just beyond the broken stockade, a mocking screech that split the darkness. The horse reared.

A fire had already been lit at the break in the wall, and some hunters ran towards it, spears ready.

They stopped.

On the further side there was a mounted shape in the darkness, and two pairs of eyes. One was a sullen red, one pair shimmered green. They stared unblinking over the flames at the villagers.

Glurk snatched a spear from one of the gaping men and pushed his way forward.

'Nothing but a snarg,' he growled, and threw. The spear struck something, but the green eyes only grew brighter. There was a deep, menacing rumble from an unseen throat.

'Be off! Go back to your lair!'

Pismire ran forward with a blazing stick in his hand, and hurled it at the eyes.

They blinked and were gone. With them went the

spell. Cries went up and, ashamed of their fear, the hunters surged forward. 'Stop!' shouted Pismire. 'Idiots! You'll chase out into the dark after that, with your bone spears? That was a black snarg. Not like the brown ones you get around here! You know the stories? They're from the furthest Corners! From the Unswept Regions!'

From the north, from the white cliff of the Woodwall itself, came again the cry of a snarg. This time it did not die away, but stopped abruptly.

Pismire stared north for a second, then turned to Glurk and Snibril. 'You have been found,' he said. 'That was what brought this horse here, fear of the snargs. And fear of the snargs is nothing to be ashamed of. Fear of snargs like that is common sense. Now they have discovered the village you can't stay. They'll come every night until one night you won't fight back hard enough. Leave tomorrow. Even that might be too late.'

'We can't just—' Glurk began.

'You can. You must. Fray is back, and all the things that come after. Do you understand?'

'No,' said Glurk.

'Then trust me,' said Pismire. 'And hope that you never *do* have to understand. Have you ever known me be wrong?'

Glurk considered. 'Well, there was that time when you said—'

'About *important* things?'

'No. I suppose not.' Glurk looked worried. 'But we've never been frightened of snargs. We can deal with snargs. What's special about these?'

'The things that ride on them,' said Pismire.

'There was another pair of eyes,' said Glurk uncertainly.

'Worse than snargs,' said Pismire. 'Got much worse weapons than teeth and claws. They've got brains.'

Chapter 2

'Well, that's the lot. Come on,' said Glurk, taking a last look at the ruins of the hut.

'Just a minute,' said Snibril.

His possessions fitted easily into one fur pack, but he rummaged through them in case anything had been left behind. There was a bone knife with the carved wooden handle, and a spare pair of boots. Then there was a coil of bowstrings, and another bag of arrowheads, a piece of lucky dust and, right at the bottom, Snibril's fingers closed round a lumpy bag. He lifted it out carefully, taking care not to damage its contents, and opened it. Two, five, eight, nine. All there, their varnish catching the light as he moved his fingers.

'Huh,' said Glurk, 'I don't know why you bother with them. Another bag of arrowheads would fill the space better.'

Snibril shook his head, and held up the coins which gleamed with varnish.

They had been shaped from the red wood of the Chairleg mines. On one side each coin carried a carving of the Emperor's head. They were Tarnerii, the coins of the Dumii, and they had cost many skins at Tregon Marus. In fact they *were* skins, if you looked at it like that, or pots or knives or spears. At least, so Pismire said.

Snibril never quite understood this, but it seemed that

so great was the Dumii's love for their Emperor they would give and take the little wooden pictures of him in exchange for skins and fur. At least, so Pismire said. Snibril wasn't sure that Pismire understood finance any more than he did.

The two of them made their way to the carts. It was less than a day since Fray had come. But what a day . . .

Arguments, mostly. The richer Munrungs hadn't wanted to leave, especially since no-one had a clear idea of where they would go. And Pismire had gone off somewhere, on business of his own.

Then, in the middle of the morning, they had heard snarg cries in the south. Someone saw shadows gliding among the hairs. Someone else said he saw eyes peering over the stockade.

After that, the arguments stopped. The Munrungs were used to travelling, as people suddenly pointed out. They moved around every year or so, to better hunting grounds. They'd been planning this move for months, probably. It wasn't as if they were running away, everyone said. No-one could say they were running away. They were *walking* away. Quite slowly.

Before mid-afternoon the area inside the stockade was filled with carts, cows and people carrying furniture. Now the bustle was over, and they all waited for Glurk. His cart was the finest, a family heirloom, with a curved roof covered with furs. It needed four ponies to pull it; huts were things you built to last a year or so, but carts were what you handed down to your grandchildren.

Behind it a string of pack ponies, laden with the Orkson wealth in furs, waited patiently. Then came the lesser carts, none as rich as the Orkson cart, though some almost equalled it. After them came the poorer handcarts, and the families that could only afford one pony and one-third shares in a cow. And last came the people on foot. It seemed to Snibril that those who carried all their personal goods in one hand looked a bit more cheerful than those who were leaving half theirs behind.

Now they needed Pismire. Where was he?

'Isn't he here?' said Glurk. 'Well, he knows we're going. He'll be along. I don't think he'd expect us to wait.'

'I'm going on ahead to find him,' said Snibril shortly.

Glurk opened his mouth to warn his brother and then thought better of it.

'Well, tell him we'll be moving along towards Burnt End, along the old tracks,' he said. 'Easy place to defend tonight, if it comes to it.'

Glurk waited until the last straggler had left the stockade, and then dragged the gate across. Anyone could get in through the broken walls, but Glurk still felt that the gates should be shut. That was more . . . proper. It suggested that they might come back one day.

Snibril was trotting up the road ahead of the procession. He rode the white horse, a little inexpertly, but with determination. The horse had been named Roland, after an uncle. No-one questioned his right to name it, or to own it. The Munrungs, on the whole, agreed with Dumii laws, but finders-keepers was one of the oldest laws of all.

A little way on he turned off the road, and soon the dazzling white wooden cliff of the Woodwall rose above the hairs. Roland's hooves made no sound on the thick dust that lay about, and the Carpet closed in. Snibril felt the great immensity of it all around him stretching far beyond the furthermost limits of the Empire. And if the Dumii road might lead to distant places, where might this old track lead?

He sat and watched it sometimes, on quiet nights. The Munrungs moved around a lot, but always in the same area. The road was always around, somewhere. Pismire talked about places like the Rug, the Hearth and

24

the Edge. Faraway places with strange-sounding names. Pismire had been everywhere, seen things Snibril would never see. He told good stories.

Several times Snibril thought he heard other hooves nearby. Or were they black paws? Roland must have heard them too, for he trotted along smartly, always on the edge of a canter.

Dust had drifted up between the hairs here, forming deep mounds where herbs and ferns grew thickly and made the air heavy with their scent. The path seemed to grow drowsy, and wound aimlessly among the dust mounds for a while. It opened out into a clearing right by the south face of the Woodwall.

It had dropped from the sky, many years before. It was a day's march long, and a good hour's walk wide. Half of it had been burned – unimaginably burned. Pismire said there had been one or two others, elsewhere in the far reaches of the Carpet, but he used the Dumii word: *matchstick*.

Pismire lived in a shack near the old wood quarry. There were a few pots lying around the door. Some thin half-wild goats skipped out of the way as Roland trotted into the clearing. Pismire was not there. Nor was his little pony.

But a freshly-tanned snarg skin was hanging by the cave. And someone was lying on a heap of ferns by a small fire, with his hat pulled down over his face. It was a high hat that might once have been blue, but time had turned it into a shapeless felt bag about the colour of smoke.

His clothes looked as though they had gathered them-selves round him for warmth. A tattered brown cloak was rolled under his head as a pillow.

Snibril left Roland in the shade of the hairs and drew his knife. He crept towards the sleeper and made to raise his hat brim with the knifepoint.

25

There was a blur of activity. It ended with Snibril flat on his back, his own knife pressed to his throat, the stranger's tanned face inches from his own.

The eyes opened. He's just waking up, Snibril thought through his terror. He started moving while he was still asleep!

'Mmm? Oh, a Munrung,' said the stranger, half to himself. 'Harmless.' He stood up.

Snibril forgot to be frightened in his haste to be offended.

'Harmless!'

'Well, by comparison to things like that,' said the stranger, indicating the skin. 'Pismire said one of you might show up.'

'Where is he?'

'Gone off to Tregon Marus. He should be back soon.'

'Who are you?'

'I like the name Bane.'

He was clean-shaven, unusual in anyone but young Dumii boys, and his red-gold hair was bound up in a plait down his back. Although in some ways he did not appear much older than Snibril himself, his face was hard and lined except for his grin. At his belt hung a fierce-looking short sword, and there was a spear beside his pack.

'I was following mouls,' he said, and saw the blankness in Snibril's face. 'Creatures. From the Unswept Regions, originally. Nasty pieces of work. They ride around on these things.'

He indicated the skin again.

'Weren't you afraid of the eyes?'

Bane laughed, and picked up his spear.

Then Pismire was with them, the rangy figure riding into the clearing, long legs almost touching the ground on either side of his pony. The old man showed no surprise that Snibril was there.

26

'Tregon Marus has fallen,' he said slowly. Bane groaned.

'I mean *fallen*,' said Pismire. 'Destroyed. The temples, the walls, everything. And snargs everywhere in the ruins. Fray has crushed the town. It was at the epicentre – right underneath,' he went on wearily. 'It has been a long, horrible day. Where've the tribe gone? Burnt End? Good enough. Very defensible situation. Come on.'

Bane had a small pony, grazing among the hairs. They set off, keeping close to the wooden cliff.

'But what *is* Fray?' said Snibril. 'I remember you telling stories about old times . . . but that was long ago. Some kind of monster. Not something real.'

'The mouls worship it,' said Bane. 'I'm . . . something of an expert.'

Snibril looked puzzled. The Munrungs didn't have gods. Life was complicated enough as it was.

'I have theories,' said Pismire. 'I've read some old books. Never mind about the stories. They're just metaphors.'

'Interesting lies,' translated Bane.

'More like . . . ways of telling things without having to do much explaining. Fray is some kind of force. There were people who used to know more, I think. There were old stories about old cities that suddenly vanished. Just legends, now. Oh, dear. So much gets forgotten. Written down and then lost.'

The little old tracks that ran everywhere in the Carpet did not go straight, like the road, but wound in and out of the hairs like serpents. Any traveller who walked them, and few did, rarely met anyone else. Yet the paths were never overgrown. The Dumii said that they had been made by Peloon, the god of journeys. The Munrungs privately held that the Carpet itself had made them in some mysterious way, although they didn't say this in front of the

Dumii. They didn't have any gods themselves but were generally polite about those belonging to other people.

Beneath the rugged tip of the Woodwall that was called Burnt End the track divided, going west and north. Glurk stopped his cart and looked up at the burnt, black crags. For a moment he thought he saw a movement high above. He sniffed the air.

'I have forebodings,' he told his wife. 'We'll wait for Snibril.'

He jumped down from the cart and walked back along the track. There it was again, something scrambling away . . . no, just a shadow. Glurk sniffed again, then shook himself. This was no way to behave, jumping at shadows. He cupped his hands round his mouth. 'Gather the carts round in a circle,' he cried. 'We'll camp here.'

If you could put up with the unpleasantness and the ash, Burnt End was a safe place to be. The hairs had broken, when the Woodwall fell on to the Carpet, so there was not much cover for attackers. And the sheer white wood wall on one side reduced the chances of an attack. But the feel of the place was unsettling. Glurk bullied the tribe until the carts formed a wall, ponies and cattle penned inside. He ordered an armed man to sit on top of every cart, and set others to lighting fires and readying the camp for the night.

Keep 'em busy. That was one of the three rules of being chief that old Grimm had passed on to him. Act confidently, never say 'I don't know', and when all else fails, keep 'em busy. He'd hunted around Burnt End before, and the deathliness around the blackened wood could be unnerving even at the best of times. The only thing to do was work, laugh loudly or sing or march about with spears, before everyone's fears got the better of them.

Soon, cooking fires sprang up within the ring. Glurk climbed on top of his cart, and peered back down the track. Fires got seen by . . . things. Yet there was nothing like it to embolden the heart, and a hot meal did wonders for the courage. Were snargs out there? Well, they could deal with snargs. They had always been about, the nasty cowardly things. Snargs had just enough brains to know not to attack a village. They preferred to track the lone traveller, if the odds were high enough. Glurk didn't like the change.

After a while Glurk climbed down and took his hunting knife from under the seat. It was carved out of a snarg's thighbone and as good as a sword if it had to be. He thrust it into his belt, and accepted a bowl of soup from his wife.

Night wore on, and the guards nodded. Outside the bright ring deeper shadows padded among the hairs . . . and it seemed as though, around the ring of light, a darker ring had grown.

They attacked to the south of the ring. There was a howl. Then a cart rocked. Its guard leapt for his life. It was Gurth, Glurk's eldest son.

'All arm! All arm! Hold the ring!' cried Glurk, and leapt across the fire with a spear in either hand. One he hurled as he ran, and he heard it hit.

These were *not* like the snargs he knew, came a cold thought out of his mind. They were daring to attack, and they carried men on their backs, or things like men at least, with green eyes and long teeth. For a moment Glurk hesitated, and an arrow grazed his arm.

Horses screamed and pulled the picket stakes out of the ground, stampeding through the running people.

Glurk saw another cart go over, and then above him loomed a snarg with a shining collar. There was a roar, and a crash, and . . . darkness spread along his arm, and drifted across his mind like nightfall.

The fires made a beacon for the three as they led their mounts down from the hidden path.

'We should head into the Empire,' said Pismire. 'Things won't be any—'

He stopped. Bane was drawing his sword. He dismounted quietly, and inched forward. With his free hand he motioned Pismire to go on talking.

'And of course Ware is so nice at this time of year,' said Pismire hurriedly, 'And there are many interesting byways and historic—'

'Have you known Bane long?' said Snibril, watching the stranger walk warily ahead.

'He's an old friend.

'But who is—'

Bane took one step forward, then whirled round and brought his sword whistling down into the shadows at his side. There was a grunt, and a body fell silently across the path, a crude black sword dropping from its hands.

Snibril gasped, and drew back. It wore armour of black leather, sewn with bone rings. At first sight the figure was manlike but when Snibril went closer he saw the hairy pelt and paws, and the long animal face.

'Mouls,' said Bane. 'I can smell 'em!'

'We must make haste!' said Pismire. 'They never move alone!'

'But it's like a human!' said Snibril. 'I thought there were only monsters and animals in the Unswept Regions.'

'Or a cross between the two,' said Bane.

The distant fires were blotted out for an instant, and a snarg cried.

Before it had died away Snibril was in Roland's saddle and away, the others in close pursuit. There was shouting up ahead, and black shapes were moving across the light. As they entered the clearing and the broken ring of carts Snibril felt the horse bunch itself together for the leap.

He clung on tightly as they cleared a cart's roof with some inches to spare and landed, lightly, inside the ring.

His arrival was hardly noticed in the battle that flowed around him.

In one place the fallen carts were on fire, and that stopped the creatures. But some had broken through, and each was roaring at the people that slashed at it.

Glurk lay still beneath one huge paw of a snarg, the biggest Snibril had ever seen. The great burning eyes moved, and saw Snibril. He wanted to run, but the horse did not budge. The rider on the snarg's back had also seen him. It grinned unpleasantly.

Snibril slipped from the horse's back and picked up Glurk's spear. It was heavy – Glurk went in for spears that other people could barely lift, let alone throw. He held it cautiously, keeping the point aimed directly at the snarg.

The snarg and its rider turned to follow him as he moved around. He could see the huge creature tensing itself to spring.

And he could see Roland. He'd sidled in a half circle, and now the snarg and its rider were behind the horse. Roland's tail twitched.

And he kicked. Both hooves struck together.

The rider sailed past Snibril's shoulder. He was dead already. No-one could look like that and still be alive.

The snarg growled in astonishment, glared at Snibril, and leapt.

You should never have to chase prey, Pismire had always said. With proper observation and care, you should be waiting for them.

Snibril didn't even think. He left the butt end of the spear wedged in the ground, and held on tightly. The snarg realized that it had done something stupid when it was in mid-air, but by then it was too late, because it was hurling itself not at some weak creature but at a spearhead . . .

That was the first battle.

Chapter 3

When Snibril awoke the night was nearly past. He was lying by a dying fire, a pelt covering him. He felt warm and aching. He shut his eyes again, hurriedly.

'You're awake,' said Bane, who was sitting with his back against a barrel and his hat, as usual, over his eyes. Roland was tethered to a nearby hair.

Snibril sat up and yawned. 'What happened? Is everyone all right?'

'Oh yes. At least, what you would call all right. You Munrungs are difficult to kill. But plenty were injured, your brother the worst, I fear. Mouls rely on poison on their swords, and they cause a . . . a sleep that you don't wake up from. Pismire is with him now. No, stay there. If anyone can cure him, then Pismire can. It won't help to have you under his feet. Besides,' he added quickly, when he saw the look in Snibril's eyes, 'how about you? We had to pull you out from under that creature.'

Snibril murmured something, and looked around him. The camp was as peaceful as a camp could be, which was to say the early dawn was filled with noises and shouts, and the sounds of people. And they were cheerful sounds, with a note of defiance.

The attack had been beaten off. For a moment with first light glimmering in the hairs, the Munrungs felt in the mood to take on Fray and all his snargs. Some, like

Bane, who never seemed to sleep, had stayed up by their fires, and early breakfasts were being cooked.

Without saying a word Bane raked a bundle out of the ashes. Warm smells rose from it. 'Haunch of snarg, baked in its own juices,' he said, slitting the burnt outer crust. 'I killed the owner myself, I'm pleased to say.'

'Protein is where you find it. I will have a piece with no fat on it,' said Pismire, stepping down from the Orkson cart.

Snibril saw the weariness in the old man's face. His herb bag lay beside him, almost empty. Pismire ate in silence for a while, and then wiped his mouth.

'He's as strong as a horse,' he said in answer to their unspoken question. 'The gods of all large amiable creatures must have been present at his birth, whether he believes in them or not. He'll still be weak, though, until the poison has completely gone. He should stay in bed for at least two days, so I told Bertha six. Then he'll fret and bully her into letting him up the day after tomorrow, and feel a lot better for having outwitted me. Positive thinking, that's the style.'

He looked at Snibril. 'What about you? You might not have escaped half so easily. Oh, I know it's useless to say all this,' he added, catching Bane's grin, 'but I wish that the people who sing about the deeds of heroes would think about the people who have to clear up after them.'

He held up his herb bag. 'And with this,' he said. 'Just different types of dust, a few useful plants. That's not medicine. That's just a way of keeping people amused while they're ill. We've lost such a lot.'

'You said that before,' said Snibril. 'What have we lost?'

'Knowledge. Proper medicine. Books. Carpography. People get lazy. Empires, too. If you don't look after knowledge, it goes away. Look at this.'

33

He threw down what looked like a belt, made up of seven different coloured squares, linked together with thongs.

'That was made by wights. Go on . . . ask me.'

'I think I've heard them mentioned . . . wights?' said Snibril obediently.

'You see? A tribe. In the old days. *The* tribe. The first Carpet people. The ones who crossed the Tiles and brought back fire. They quarried wood at the Woodwall. They found out how to melt varnish off *achairleg*. Don't see them so much nowadays, but they used to be around a lot, pushing these big varnish-boilers from tribe to tribe, it's amazing the stuff they could make out of it . . . Anyway, they used to make these belts. Seven different substances, you see. Carpet hair, bronze from the High Gate Land, varnish, wood, dust, sugar and grit. Every wight had to make one.'

'Why?'

'To prove they could. Mysticism. Of course, that was long ago. I haven't see wights for years. And now their belts turn up as collars on these . . . things. We've lost so much. We wrote too much down, and forgot it.' He shook his head. 'I'm going to have a nap. Wake me up when we leave.' He wandered off to one of the carts and pulled a blanket over his head.

'What did he mean?' said Snibril.

'A nap,' said Bane. 'It's like a short sleep.'

'I *mean* about writing down too much. Who wrote down too much? What does that mean?'

For the first time since Snibril had met him, Bane looked uncomfortable.

'That's up to him to tell you,' he said. 'Everyone has . . . things they remember.'

Snibril watched him patting Roland absently on the muzzle. Who was Bane, if it came to that? He seemed to generate a feeling that made it hard to ask. He looked

like a wild man, but there was something about him . . .
It seemed to Snibril that if a pot that was about to boil
over had arms and legs, that would be Bane. Every move
he made was deliberate and careful, as if he'd rehearsed
it beforehand. Snibril wasn't sure if Bane was a friend.
He hoped so. He'd be a terrible enemy.

He lay back with the belt in his lap and thought of
wights. Eventually he slept. At least, it seemed like
sleep, but he thought that he could still hear the camp
around him and see the outline of Burnt End across the
clearing. But he wondered afterwards. It seemed like a
dream. He saw, in a little blurred picture hanging in the
smoke-scented air, the Carpet. He was flying through
the hairs, well above the dust. It was night-time and
very dark although, oddly enough, he could see quite
clearly. He drifted over grazing herds, a group of hooded
figures – wights! – pushing a cart, a sleeping village . . .
and then, as if he been drawn to this spot, to a tiny
figure walking among the hairs. As he drifted down
towards it, it became a person, all in white. Everything
about it was white. It turned and looked up at him,
the first creature he had seen who seemed to know he
was there . . . and he sank towards those pale, watchful
eyes . . .

He woke suddenly, and the picture faded, while he sat
up clutching the seven squares tightly in both hands.

A little later they broke camp, with Pismire driving the
leading cart.

Glurk lay inside, white and shaken, but strong enough
to curse colourfully every time they went over a bump.
Sometimes Fray rumbled far off in the south.

Bane and Snibril, now wearing the belt around his
waist, rode on ahead.

The Carpet was changing colour. That in itself was
not strange. Around the Woodwall the hairs were dark

green and grey, but west in Tregon Marus they were a light, dusty blue. Here the green was fading to yellow, and the hairs themselves were thicker and gnarled. Some bore fruit, large prickly balls that grew right out of the trunk of the hair.

Bane cut into one with his knife, and showed Snibril the thick sweet syrup.

Later they passed far under some kind of construction high in the hairs. Striped creatures peered down from their lofty fortress and hummed angrily as the carts passed beneath.

'They're hymetors,' called out Pismire, while the noise thrummed above their heads. 'Don't take any notice of them! They're peaceful enough if you leave them alone, but if they think you're after their honey they'll sting you!'

'Are they intelligent?' said Snibril.

'Together they are. Individually, they're stupid. Hah! The opposite of us, really. Incidentally, their stings are deadly.'

After that no-one as much as looked at a syrup ball, and Bane spent a lot of time glancing upwards with one hand on his sword.

After a while they reached a place where two tracks crossed. A cairn of grit marked the crossroads. On the cairn, their packs at their feet, sat a man and a woman. They were ragged creatures; their clothes made Bane's clean tatters look like an Emperor's robe.

They were eating cheese. Both started to back away when Bane and Snibril approached, and then relaxed.

The man wanted to talk. Words seemed to have piled up inside him.

'Camus Cadmes is my name,' he said. 'I was a hair-cutter for the sawmill in Marus there. I suppose I'm still a hair-cutter now, too, if anyone wants to employ me. Hmm? Oh. I was out marking hairs for cutting and Lydia here had brought out my dinner and then there was this sort of *heavy* feeling and then—'

And then he'd got to a point where words weren't enough, and had to be replaced by arm-waving and a look of extreme terror.

'When we got back I don't think there was a yard of wall left standing. The houses just fell in on themselves. We did what we could but . . . well, anyone who could just left. You can't rebuild from something like that. Then I heard the wolf things, and . . . we ran.'

He took the piece of meat that Snibril gave him and they ate it hungrily.

'Did no-one else escape?' said Snibril.

'Escape? From that? Maybe, those outside the walls. There was Barlen Corronson with us until yesterday. But he went after the syrup of those humming things, and they got him. Now we're going east. I've got family that way. I hope.'

They gave them new clothes and full packs, and sent them on their way. The couple hurried off, almost as fearful of the Munrungs as they were of the other sudden terrors of the Carpet.

'Everyone ran,' said Snibril. 'We're all running away.'

'Yes,' said Bane looking down the west path with an odd expression. 'Even these.' He pointed, and there coming slowly up the path, was a heavy wagon drawn by a line of bent, plodding figures.

Chapter 4

'Wights,' said Bane. 'Don't speak to them unless they speak first.'

'I saw them last night in a dream . . .' began Snibril.

Pismire showed no surprise. 'You've got one of their belts. You know when you really work hard at something, you're really putting yourself into your work? *They* mean it.'

Snibril slipped the belt from his tunic and, without quite knowing why he did it, slipped it into his pack.

Behind them the rest of the carts slowed down and drew to the side of the path.

The wight-drawn wagon rumbled on until it reached the cairn. Both parties looked across at the others. Then a small wight left the cart and walked across to Snibril and Bane. Close to, its robe could be seen to be, not just black, but covered in a crisscross of faint grey lines. The deep hood covered its face.

'Hello,' said the wight.

'Hello,' said Bane.

'Hello,' nodded the wight again.

It stood there, and said nothing else.

'Do they understand language?' said Snibril.

'Probably,' said Pismire. 'They invented it.'

Snibril felt its steady gaze from the hidden eyes. And he felt the hardness of the belt rubbing into his back, and shifted uneasily. The wight turned its gaze on Bane.

'Tonight we eat the Feast of Bronze. You are invited. You will accept. Seven only. When the night-time fires are lit.'

'We accept,' said Bane, gravely.

The wight turned on his heel and strode back to the wagon. 'Tonight?' said Pismire. 'The Feast of Bronze? As if it was Feast of Sugar or Hair? Amazing. I thought they never invited strangers.'

'Who's invited who?' growled someone from inside the cart. There was a stamping about, and Glurk's head poked through the curtains over the front.

'You know what I said about getting up . . .' Pismire began, but since Glurk was already dressed there was very little he could do, except wink slyly at Bane and Snibril.

'Wights? I thought they were just a children's story,' Glurk said, after it had been explained to him. 'Still, it's a free meal. What's wrong with that? To tell the truth I don't know more'n a scrap about them, but I never heard of a bad wight.'

'I'd hardly heard of wights at all until now,' said Snibril.

'Ah, but you weren't alive when old Granddad was,' said Glurk. 'He told me he met one out in the hairs once. He lent it his axe.'

'Did he get it back?' said Pismire.

'No.'

'That was a wight all right, then,' said Pismire. 'They tend to be too preoccupied to think about simple things.'

'He said it was a good axe, too.'

'There's no question of refusing to go,' said Pismire.

'That's right,' said Bane.

'But it's so easy to get things wrong. You know how sensitive they are. They've got all kinds of strange beliefs. You've got to know that, you two. Tell them, General.'

39

'Well,' said Bane, 'seven's very important to them. Seven elements in the Carpet, seven colours—'

'Tell them about the Chays.'

'I was coming to that . . . seven Chays. They're like . . . periods of time. But not regular ones. Sometimes they're short, sometimes they're long. Only the wights know how long. Remember the belt? Seven squares, and each represents a Chay. So the Chay of Salt, you see, is a time when people prosper and trade, and the Chay of Grit is when they build empires and walls . . . am I going too fast?'

General? thought Snibril. That's what Pismire said. He wasn't thinking. And a general's a chief soldier . . . and now they're all looking at me. None of them noticed!

'Hmm?' he said. He tried to recall what Bane had been saying. 'Oh . . . so tonight's Feast means we're in the Chay of Bronze, yes?'

'It means it's starting,' said Pismire. 'It's a time of war and destruction.'

Glurk coughed. 'How long does this last, then?'

'It'll last as long as the wights think it will. Don't ask me how they know. But tonight wights all over the Carpet will celebrate the Feast of Bronze. It's something to do with their memories.'

'Sounds a bit unbelievable to me,' said Glurk.

'Oh, yes. But that doesn't mean it isn't true.'

'You certainly know a lot about them,' said Snibril.

'I don't,' said Pismire, simply. 'You never know anything where wights are concerned. You remember tales, see things, pick up little bits of knowledge here and there, but you never know anything for certain.'

'All right,' said Glurk. He stood up on the driving-board of the cart. 'We'll go. Don't see we can do nothing else, anyway. Bertha'll come, and Gurth, and, let's see . . . yes, Damion Oddfoot. It strikes me that when a wight asks you to dinner you go, and that's it. In sevens.'

*   *   *

They entered the wights' little camp sheepishly, keeping together.

Wights always travelled in numbers of seven, twenty-one or forty-nine. No-one knew what happened to any wights left over. Perhaps the other ones killed and ate them, suggested Glurk, who had taken a sort of ancestral dislike to axe-stealing wights. Pismire told him to shut up.

The oldest wight in the group was the Master. There were twenty-one in this group and Pismire, looking at their cart, pointed out the big varnish-boiler on top of it. Wights specialized in smelting the varnish that was mined at the Varnisholme, the giant pillar of red wood in the north known as *achairleg* in Dumii. Then they went from village to village, selling it. Varnish could be cast into a spear head, or a knife, or just about anything.

Snibril wondered how long would it be before anyone noticed he had shoved the belt back in his pack? But he wasn't going to give it up, he told himself. They'd be bound to want it back if they saw it.

There were seven fires, close together, and three wights around each. They looked identical. How do they tell one another apart, Snibril wondered?

'Oh, there's something else I forgot to tell you,' said Pismire, as the wights busied themselves over their cooking pots. 'They have perfect memories. Um. They remember everything. That's why they find it so hard to talk to ordinary people.'

'I don't understand,' said Snibril.

'Don't be surprised if they give you answers before you've asked the question. Sometimes even *they* get confused,' Pismire went on.

'Never mind about them. *I'm* confused.'

'They remember everything, I said. *Everything*. Everything that's ever going to happen to them. Their minds

41

. . . work differently. The past and the future are all the same to them. Please try to understand what I'm saying. They remember things that *haven't happened yet.*'

Snibril's jaw dropped.

'Then we could ask them—' he began.

'No! We mustn't! Why, thank you,' Pismire continued, in a more normal voice, taking a plate from a wight, 'that looks . . . um . . . delicious.'

They ate in silence. Snibril thought: do they say nothing because they already know what it was they said? No, that can't be right – they'd have to speak now to remember having said it . . . or . . .

'I am Noral the kilnmaster,' said the wight on his left.

'My name—'

'Yes.'

'We—'

'Yes.'

'There was—'

'I know.'

'*How?*'

'You're going to tell me after dinner.'

'Oh.' Snibril tried to think. Pismire was right. It was almost impossible to hold a conversation with someone who'd already heard it once. 'You really know everything that's going to happen?' was all he could think of.

There was the trace of a smile in the depths of the hood.

'Not everything. How can anyone know everything? But a number of things I do know, yes.'

Snibril looked around desperately. Bane and Pismire were deep in conversation with wights, and were not paying him any attention.

'But . . . but . . . supposing you knew when you were going to die? Supposing a wild animal was going to attack you?'

'Yes?' said Noral politely.

'You could just make sure you weren't there?'

'Weren't there when you died?' said the wight. 'That would be a good trick.'

'No! I mean . . . you could avoid—'

'I know what you mean. But we couldn't. It's hard to explain. Or easy to explain and hard to understand. We have to follow the Thread. The one Thread. We mustn't break it.'

'Doesn't anything ever come as a surprise?' said Snibril.

'I don't know. What is a surprise?'

'Can you tell me what's going to happen to me? To all of us? You know what's been happening already. It would help a lot to know the future.'

The dark hood turned towards him.

'It wouldn't. It makes living very hard.'

'We need help,' said Snibril, in a frantic whisper. 'What's Fray? Where can we go to be safe? What should we do? Can't you tell us?'

The wight leaned closer.

'Can you keep a secret?' it said, conspiratorially.

'Yes!' said Snibril.

'*Really* keep a secret? Even though you'd give anything to tell other people? Even though it's like trying to hold a hot coal in your hand? Can you *really* keep a secret?'

'Er . . . yes.'

'Well,' said the wight, leaning back again. 'So can we.'

'But—'

'Enjoy your meal.'

'Will I?'

'Yes. You certainly did.' The wight went to turn away, and then turned back. 'And you may keep the belt.'

'Oh. You know I've got the belt.'

43

'I do now.'

Snibril hesitated. 'Hang on,' he said, 'I only said that because you—'

'It's best if you don't try to understand,' said Noral, kindly.

Snibril ate for a while, but the questions kept bothering him.

'Listen. Everything happens,' said Noral. 'Like a Thread of the Carpet. Nothing can be changed. Even the changes are . . . already part of the future. That's all you need to know.'

It was a strange meal. You could never be certain if the person you were talking to was listening to what you were going to say in ten minutes' time. It only cheered up a bit when one of the wights gave Glurk an axe. It was his grandfather's, although the handle and the blade had been replaced a few times.

Bane and Pismire were quiet when the travellers went back to their carts.

'Did they tell *you* anything?' asked Snibril.

'No,' said Pismire. 'They never do. But . . .'

'It's the way they acted,' said Bane. 'They can't help it.'

'They don't like what it is they're not telling us,' said Pismire.

Chapter 5

A week passed. The carts went on northward. Around them the Carpet changed. On either side of the narrow track the hairs towered up, and now they were deep red. The fluff bushes, too, even the dust briars, grew in every shade of red.

To Snibril it seemed as though they were walking through a great fire that had been frozen suddenly. But it was cool and peaceful and at night, for the first time since they had left the village, they heard no snargs.

And that, of course, made people want to stop. 'At least for a few weeks,' said Cadmic Hargolder, the spearmaker, when several villagers came to Glurk's cart one evening. 'They've probably forgotten about us, anyway, and perhaps we can go home.'

'They don't forget,' said Bane. 'Not them. Besides, we must go on. Head for Ware.'

'You two can, if you like,' said Cadmic. 'As for me . . .'

'As for us, we'll keep together, Cadmic, at least while I'm chief of this tribe,' said Glurk. 'I won't think we're safe till I'm certain the nearest moul is a long way away. Makes sense to head for Ware. Things'll be better there, you'll see. If any of you think different, well . . .'

There was something in that 'well'. It was a very deep 'well'. It was full of unspoken threats.

But there were still angry mutterings. Then they came across the moul.

It was while Snibril and Bane were walking ahead along the track, out of sight but within hearing of the carts. Snibril said little. He kept thinking about 'General'.

He'd seen Dumii officers occasionally. Not often. Tregon Marus wasn't very important. They didn't like it much, so far from home. Bane *moved* like a soldier. People called 'General' shouldn't go around looking so shabby . . . And now they were going to Ware, apparently. No-one had discussed it. Suddenly it just seemed to be happening.

Things would be all right in Ware, though. It was the most famous place in the Carpet. Better than anywhere else. Safe. There were legions and legions of soldiers there . . .

Bane was probably sensing his thoughts, but he was, unusually for him, chatting aimlessly about nothing in particular.

Neither saw the moul until they were almost on top of it. It sat astride its snarg in the middle of the track, hand halfway to sword hilt, staring straight at them with a look of terror.

Bane gave a grunt and drew his sword, then almost fell over when Snibril's arm shot out and grabbed his shoulder.

'What are you doing, you idiot?'

'*Look* at it,' said Snibril. Observe, Pismire always said, before acting . . .

The moul had not moved. Snibril crept forward. Then, reaching up, he tapped the creature on its snout. Without saying a word he pointed to the snarg's legs. Thick drifts of dust lay undisturbed around them.

There was even a film of dust on the moul. It sat there, a statue, staring blankly at nothing.

46

'How could it—' Snibril began.

'Don't know. Pismire might,' said Bane, rather roughly, because he felt a bit of a fool. 'Come on. You take its head and I'll take its legs.'

They gingerly unseated it from its snarg and carried it, still in a sitting position, back to the carts.

Snibril stuck his knife in his belt where he could reach it easily, just in case. But the moul seemed to be made out of grit.

They found Pismire already fully occupied. Glurk had been out hunting and had come back with a wild pig. Or at least the statue of one.

'There was a whole herd of these,' Glurk was saying. He tapped the pig with his spear. It went *boinnng*.

'Should go "oink",' he told them. 'Not *boinnng*.'

Pismire took Snibril's knife and rapped the moul on the chest. It went *ping*.

'Should go "Aaaggh!"' said Glurk.

'Are they dead?' asked Snibril.

'Not sure,' said Pismire, and one or two of the more nervous watchers strolled hurriedly away. 'Look.'

Snibril looked into the moul's eyes. They were wide open, and a dull black. But deep in them there was something . . . just a flicker, a tiny imprisoned spark in the pool of darkness.

Snibril shuddered and turned away, meeting Pismire's steady gaze. 'Amazing. Premature fossilization. And I didn't know there were any termagants in these parts. Tonight's guards had better be picked for their hearing.'

'Why?' said Glurk.

'Because they'd better wear blindfolds.'

'Why?'

There was a shout, and Yrno Berius came running up with one of his hounds in his arms.

'Heard him bark,' he gasped. 'Went to find him, found him like this.'

47

Pismire examined it.

'Lucky,' he said, vaguely.

'I don't think so!' said Yrno.

'Not him,' said Pismire. 'You.'

The dog was still in a crouched position, ready to spring, with its teeth bared and its tail between its legs.

'What's a termagant?' asked Snibril, finally looking away.

'There have been quite a lot of descriptions of their back view,' said Pismire. 'Unfortunately, no-one who's looked at one from the front has been able to tell us much. They get turned to stone. No-one knows why. Amazing. Haven't heard of any for years. Thought they'd all died out.'

And that evening Pismire himself nearly died out. He always held that goat's milk was essential for a philosopher, so not long after they had left the Woodwall he had bought a nanny goat from Glurk's small flock.

Her name was Chrystobella, and she hated Pismire with deep animal hatred. When she didn't feel like being milked, which was twice a day, it was part of camp life to watch her skitter between carts with a hot and breathless Pismire cursing in pursuit. Mothers would waken their children to come and watch. It was a sight they'd remember for the rest of their lives, they said.

This time she hurled out between the carts and into the hairs with a taunting bleat. Pismire scrambled after her, leapt down into the darkness, and tripped over her . . .

Something backed hastily into the shadows, with a faint jingling.

Pismire came back holding the statue of a goat. He put it down silently, and tapped its muzzle.

It went *ping*.

'Should go "blaaarrrrt",' said Pismire. '*No-one* go out of the camp tonight.'

That night ten men stood around the ring, their eyes

48

tightly shut. Snibril was among them and he stood by Roland, who wore blinkers.

And they did it the next night, too. And the one after that, after a cow belonging to the widow Mulluck started to go *ping* when it should have gone 'mmmmmyaooooo'.

No-one wanted to move on. They didn't break camp but, without anyone actually giving any orders, brought the wagons into a tighter circle.

Once or twice they thought they heard jingling noises.

And then, on the third night, Snibril was on guard by one of the carts, almost asleep, when he heard a shuffling noise behind him. Something big was in the bushes. He could hear it breathing.

He was about to spin around when he heard the jingle of metal.

It's here, he thought. It's right behind me. If I turn around, I'll be turned to stone. But if I don't turn around, will I be turned to supper?

He stood quite still for a hundred years or so . . .

After a while the shuffling grew fainter, and he risked the briefest look. In the dim light he could see something bulky, at least twice as tall as he was, disappearing among the hairs.

I ought to call everyone, he thought. But they'll run around and shout and give one another orders and trip over things, and then it will have long gone. But I've got to do something. Otherwise we'll soon have a statue that goes *ping* when it should go 'Hello'.

He found Roland, and quickly put his bridle on. There was no time for the saddle. And then he led the horse, very quietly in the direction of the jingling.

Chapter 6

The termagant was so old that he could not remember a time when he'd been young. He could dimly remember when there had been other termagants, but he was strong then, and had driven them out.

Later on there had been a people who had worshipped him and built a temple for him to live in, thinking that he was some kind of a god. They had worshipped him because he was so destructive, which is what often happens, but that sort of religion never works out in the long term; after he had turned many of them to statues the ones that were left had fled and left him in his temple.

He had no company now. Even the wild creatures kept away from the temple. In vain did he wander abroad and call out to his people in the south. There was no answer. He probably was the last termagant in the Carpet.

Sometimes he went to find some company. Anything would do. Just some other living things. He wouldn't even eat them. But it never worked. He only had to get near and they'd get stiff and cold and unfriendly for some reason.

So he tramped back to his ruined temple, his tail dragging behind him. He was almost at the door before he smelt the smell, the forgotten smell of company.

Snibril had reached the ruined temple just before. He felt Roland's hooves trot over hard wooden paving. Around him, lit by a faint glow, he could see fallen walls, littered with statues. Some were holding out boxes and bowing low, some were crouched back, hands to their eyes. There were small wild animals there, too . . . unmoving.

In the centre of the temple there was a ruined altar, and that was the source of the glow. On it and around it were piled treasures. There were stones of salt and black jet, boxes of clear varnish and red wood, carved bone rings, crowns of bronze, all heaped anyhow.

By the treasure was another statue. It was a small warrior, hardly half Snibril's height. Magnificent moustaches hung down almost to its waist. In one hand it held a sword and round shield, in the other a necklace of glittering salt crystals. Its face was turned up in an expression of surprise. A fluff creeper had crept across the floor to him, giving him a necklace of living red flowers.

Snibril tethered Roland to a pillar, and shuddered.

Someone else had tethered their mount there before him. It still stood there. It looked like a pony, but it was no larger than a Munrung dog, and had six legs.

Snibril could have picked it up in both hands. There it stood, wearing a thin coat of dust. Roland lowered his head and sniffed at the still muzzle, puzzled. Snibril padded over to the mound of treasure and stared in awe. There were even coins there, not Tarnerii, but large wooden discs bearing strange signs. There were heavy swords, and chests of carved grit, set with salt gems. He stood and stared, and saw the warrior out of the corner of his eye.

Hand reaching out . . .

That was why he had come. And the termagant had found him.

There was a jingling noise. Snibril saw a reflection in the statue's polished shield. It showed something scaly and very nearly shapeless.

51

It's in the doorway, Snibril thought. Right behind me . . .

But if I turn around . . .

He unhooked the shield, holding it up so that he could see over his shoulder.

The termagant jingled. Around its leathery neck were chains of varnish and red wood. Every claw was aglitter with rings. Bracelets were threaded on the scaly tail. Every time it moved its big beaked head it sent a little tinkling noise echoing round the temple.

It peered at the altar and sniffed. Even in the shield the eyes frightened Snibril. They were large and misty blue, not frightening at all. Eyes you could get lost in, he thought, and turn to stone.

Roland gave a whinny, but it ended in mid-air. Then there was another statue in the cold hall.

Snibril's senses screamed at him to turn round and face the creature, but he stood still and thought desperately. The termagant began to jingle towards him.

Snibril turned, holding the polished shield before his eyes. Under it he could see the termagant's feet scraping towards him. They were bony and clawed. And they *didn't* stop . . .

It ought to have turned to stone. It saw itself! So much for bright ideas, he thought. And it was the only one I had.

He started to back away. And then the termagant did stop. For it had seen another termagant. There, in the shield, a scaly green face looked back at it. A necklace hung over one ear. For a moment the creature had found company. Then, because he was shaking with fear, Snibril tilted the shield. The face vanished.

After a moment of shocked silence the termagant let out a howl of anguish that echoed around the hairs. A massive foot stamped. Then the creature collapsed on the floor, put its paws over its eyes, and began to sob. Every

52

now and then it'd drum its back feet on the floor. The sobs started at the tail end, by the look of it, and got bigger and bigger as they gulped their way up towards the mouth.

It wasn't only terrifying. It was also embarrassing. Nothing should have that many tears in it.

Snibril watched the pool of tears spread out over the floor, and touch the statue of a hairhog by the wall. It twitched its nose. Wider and wider went the pool. Some statues awoke as it touched them, but some of the oldest, all covered in dust and creepers, stood unchanged. Little creatures swam valiantly to freedom between their ankles.

Snibril scooped up the tears in the shield and splashed them over Roland. Then it was the turn of the little pony, which stared up at Snibril in amazement. He ran to the warrior by the treasure, and drenched him.

Nothing happened for a moment. An eyelid flickered. The hand with the necklace started to move. The little warrior was suddenly very much alive. He dropped the necklace and glowered at Snibril. 'Kone's Bones, where did you spring from?'

Then he saw the termagant in its pool of tears. His hand went to his throat, and found the creeper.

He looked thoughtfully at Snibril.

'How long have I been here, stranger?'

'I don't know. This is the third year after the second Counting in the reign of the Emperor Targon at Ware,' said Snibril.

'You're a Dumii?' said the released statue, unwinding the creeper.

'Sort of.'

'I'm not,' said the little warrior, proudly. 'We don't Count. But I've heard of Targon. Before I came here it was the twenty-second year of his rule.'

'Then you must have been here a year,' said Snibril.

'A year . . . a year away,' said the warrior. 'Far too long.'

He bowed solemnly. 'A thousand pardons, stranger,' he said. 'You shall be rewarded for this. I, Brocando, Son of Broc, Lord of Jeopard, King of the Deftmenes, promise you that. Yes. Rewarded.'

'I didn't do it for any reward,' said Snibril. 'I just wanted the thing to stop turning everything into statues.'

'What brings you this far from home, then?' Brocando asked, with a glint in his eye. 'The treasure, eh?'

'No ... look, do you think we'd better go?' said Snibril, glancing at the termagant again. 'It might get up.'

Brocando flourished his sword.

'One year of my life!' he shouted. 'I'll make it pay for that!'

Snibril looked at the creature again. It was lying quite still.

'I don't think there's much more you can do to it,' he said. 'It looks miserable enough to me.'

Brocando hesitated. 'You may be right,' he said. 'There is no revenge on a witless beast. As for this . . .' he swept his arm over the shimmering heap, 'I have lost the taste for it. Let it lie here.' He sniffed. 'It is in my mind that such things as these are fit only for termagants. Mind you, that necklace looks rather . . . no . . .'

Snibril had seen one or two items that he rather liked, and by the look of him Brocando could leave treasure behind because he had lots more at home, but he felt that it would look bad to argue.

With a soft jingling the termagant raised its head and opened its eyes. Snibril went to lift his shield and it slipped out of his hands, rolling down the steps.

The termagant stopped it clumsily with a claw and turned it awkwardly until it could see itself again.

To Snibril's amazement it began to coo at its reflection, and lay back again with the mirror cuddled in its arms. And then the termagant, with a clank, died peacefully in the temple that had been built for it time out of mind.

Often, later, it was said by minstrels and wandering story-tellers that the termagant died when it caught sight of itself in the mirror. Never believe what you hear in songs. They put in any old thing if they think it sounds better. They said that its reflected glance turned it to a statue. But the death of the termagant was more complicated than that. Most things are.

They dragged it up the steps and buried it under the altar stone. Snibril remembered Chrystobella and the other animals back at the camp, and collected some of the tear puddle into a small jewel-case from the heap. The remaining statues they left where they were.

'In the past they worshipped the termagants, so the story goes,' said Brocando. 'They were a cruel race. Let them remain. For justice.'

'Actually . . .' Snibril began, as they rode away, 'I wouldn't mind just a *small* reward. If you happen to have one you want to give away. One you don't need.'

'Certainly!'

'My tribe needs somewhere to stay for a while. To repair the wagons, and so on. Somewhere where we don't have to look over our shoulders all the time.'

'Easily granted. My city is yours. My people will welcome you.'

'Are they all small like you?' said Snibril, without thinking.

'We Deftmenes are *correctly-built*,' said Brocando. 'It's no business of ours if everyone else is ridiculously overgrown.'

After a while, as they neared the Munrung's camp, Snibril said: 'You know, I don't think you've lost a year. If you were a statue, time couldn't have passed for you. In a way, you've gained a year. Everyone else is a year older, except you.'

Brocando thought about this. 'Does that mean I still give you the reward?' he said.

'I think so,' said Snibril.

'Right.'

55

Chapter 7

They arrived at the camp just in time to stop the search party that was setting out. Brocando immediately became the centre of attention, something which he enjoyed and was obviously used to. Snibril was more or less forgotten. More or less . . .

'Where have you been?' asked Pismire, relieved and angry. 'Wandering off like that! Don't you know there are mouls about?'

'I'm sorry,' said Snibril, 'Things just happened.'

'Well, never mind now,' said Pismire. 'What's happening over there, now? Doesn't anyone of your muddle-headed people know how to welcome a king?'

'I don't think so,' said Snibril. 'He's quite brave and a bit excitable and doesn't really listen to what you say.'

'Sounds like a king to me, right enough,' said Pismire.

Brocando was in the centre of a crowd of chattering, staring Munrungs, beaming benevolently.

'There I was,' he was saying. 'One step away from the treasure, when, jingle! There it was, behind me. So . . .'

Pismire elbowed his way through the crowd, removed his hat, bowed till his beard touched the ground, and stuck there, confronting a surprised Brocando with a tangle of white locks.

'Greeting, oh King,' said the old man. 'Honoured are we that so great a son of so noble an ancestry should deem us worthy to . . . er . . . worthy. All we have is at your disposal, valiant sir. I am Pismire, a humble philosopher. This is . . .'

He snapped his fingers wildly at Glurk, who was standing open-mouthed at the spectacle of Pismire, still bent double in front of the dwarf warrior.

'Come on, come on. Protocol is very important. Bow down to the king!'

'What's a king?' said Glurk, looking round blankly.

'Show some respect,' said Pismire.

'What for? Snibril rescued *him*, didn't he?'

Snibril saw Bane, standing at the back of the crowd with folded arms and a grim expression. He hadn't liked school in Tregon Marus, but he'd learned some things. The Dumii didn't like kings. They preferred Emperors, because they were easier to get rid of.

And on the way back from the temple he'd asked Brocando what he'd meant when he said his people didn't Count. It meant they had nothing to do with the Dumii.

'Hate them,' Brocando had said, bluntly. 'I'd fight them because they straighten roads, and number things, and make maps of places that shouldn't be mapped. They turn everything into things to Count. They'd make the hairs of the carpet grow in rows if they could. And worst of all . . . they obey orders. They'd rather obey orders than think. That's how their Empire *works*. Oh, they're fair enough, fair fighters in battle and all that sort of thing, but they don't know how to laugh and at the end of it all it's things in rows, and orders, and all the fun out of life.'

And now he was about to be introduced to one of them.

At which point, Brocando amazed him. He walked up to Glurk and shook him warmly by the hand. When he spoke, it wasn't at all in the way he'd used in the temple.

57

It was the kind of voice that keeps slapping you on the back all the time.

'So you're the chieftain, are you?' he said. 'Amazing! Your brother here told me all about you. It must be an incredibly difficult job. Highly skilled, too, I shouldn't wonder?'

'Oh, you know . . . you pick it up as you go along . . .' Glurk muttered, taken aback.

'I'm sure you do. I'm *sure* you do. Fascinating! And a terrible responsibility. Did you have to have some sort of special training?'

'. . . er . . . no . . . Dad died and they just gives me the spear and said, you're chief . . .' said Glurk.

'Really? We shall have to have a serious chinwag about this later on,' said Brocando. 'And this is Pismire, isn't it? Oh, do get up. I'm sure philosophers don't have to bow, what? Jolly good. And this must be . . . General Baneus Catrix, I believe.'

General! Snibril thought.

Bane nodded.

'How many years is it, your majesty?' he said.

'About five, I think,' said the king. 'Better make that six, in fact.'

'You know each other?' said Snibril.

'Oh, yes,' said Brocando. 'The Dumii kept sending armies to see us and suggest, most politely, that we submit and be part of their Empire. We always told them we didn't want to join. We weren't going to be Counted—'

'I think it was the paying of taxes you objected to,' said Bane, calmly.

'We did not see what we would get for our money,' said Brocando.

'You would be defended,' said Bane.

'Ah . . . but we've always been quite good at defending ourselves,' said Brocando, in a meaningful tone of voice.

58

'Against *anyone*.' He smiled. 'And then the General here was sent to suggest it to us *again*, with a little more force,' he said. 'I remember he said that he was afraid that if we did not join the Empire, there would be hardly any of us to be Counted.'

'And *you* said there'd be hardly anyone left to do the Counting,' said Bane.

Snibril looked from one to the other. He realized he was holding his breath. He let it out. 'And then what happened?' he said.

Bane shrugged. 'I didn't attack,' he said. 'I didn't see why good people should die. I went back and told the Emperor that Brocando's people would make better allies than unwilling subjects. Anyway, only a fool would attack *that* city.'

'I always wondered what he replied,' said Brocando.

Bane looked down at his ragged clothes. 'He shouted quite a lot,' he said.

There was a thoughtful pause.

'They did attack, you know, after you . . . been recalled,' said Brocando.

'Did they win?'

'No.'

'You see? Fools,' said Bane.

'I'm sorry,' said Brocando.

'You needn't be. It was only one of a number of disagreements I had with the Emperor,' said Bane.

Snibril took each of them by the shoulder. 'Anyway,' he said, 'just because you're sworn enemies doesn't mean you can't be friends, does it?'

When they were having the evening meal Glurk said to his wife: 'He's very gracious. Asked all about me. I've met a *king*. He's very important. He's called Protocol, I think.'

'Good name. Sounds *royal*,' she said.

'And Pismire's a philosopher, he says.'

'I never knew that. What's a philosopher?'

'Someone who thinks, he says,' said Glurk.

'Well, *you* think. I've often seen you sitting and think-ing.'

'I don't always think,' said Glurk conscientiously. 'Sometimes I just sits.' He sighed. 'Anyway, it's not just thinking. You've got to be able to talk about it entertainingly afterwards.'

Chapter 8

The people turned west. It was a cheerful journey to Jeopard, with Brocando riding by the leading cart. They were going somewhere that only a fool would attack.

Many of the Munrungs were frankly in awe of the small king, but Glurk was fast becoming an uncritical royalist. Brocando sensed his respectful audience, and chatted to him in that special way royalty has for commoners, which leaves the commoner feeling really cheered up without actually remembering very much about what was said to him.

Snibril jogged along on the other side of the cart, listening with half an ear for any signs of Fray and half to the Deftmene's chatter. 'And then in the north wing of the palace my ancestor, Broc, built a temple to Kone the Founder. It took the wights seven years, carving pillars of varnish and wood and laying the great mosaic of the Carpet for Broc. We're still paying them for it. The walls were set with jet and salt, the altar of red wood inlaid with bronze. Really that was the centre of the present palace, which was built by my great-grandfather, the Seventh Broc, who added the Wood Gate when he was made king. And I mustn't forget the treasure rooms. I think there's at least nine. And only the reigning king may enter. Tarma the Woodcarver himself made the Crown. Seven pointy bits, with salt crystals on each one.'

'We had a rug in our hut,' said Glurk.

61

And so it went on, Glurk eagerly following the Deftmene through the treasury and the armoury, the banqueting halls and the guest bedrooms, while the carts got nearer and nearer to Jeopard.

Gradually the Carpet changed colour again, from red to deep purple and then dark blue. They camped under blue hairs, hunted the small shelled creatures that dwelt in dust holes, and wondered if Jeopard was as good as Brocando made out because if it was, it looked as though they'd better stop eating and drinking right now so as to leave room for the feasts they were going to have.

The track began to turn into a road, not a great white road like the Dumii built, but a neatly laid track of thick planks on a bank of dust. On either side the hairs grew thinner, and Snibril noticed many stumps. That was not all. No Munrung ever planted a seed. They liked vegetables when they could get them, and knew what grew where and which hairs dropped seeds that could be eaten, but except for Pismire's private herb garden everything that grew around them grew wild. The reason was quite obvious, to a Munrung: if you planted something you had to stop and watch it grow, fight off the animals and any hungry neighbour that happened to be passing, and generally spend your time, as Glurk put it, hanging around. Vegetables to a Munrung were something to give the meat a bit of a special taste.

But in the blue land of Jabonya, around the little city of Jeopard, the Deftmenes had turned the Carpet into a garden. There were hairs there that even Pismire had not seen before, not the great sturdy trunks that crowded the rest of the Carpet, but delicate stems, their branches laden with fruit. Dust had been carefully banked up beneath them to make soil for all sorts of shrubs and vegetables. The travellers were shown ripe purple groads, that tasted of pepper and ginger, and big Master Mushrooms that could be dried and stored for years and still kept their delicate flavour. Even the track had been raised above the gardens, and small shrublike hairs grew along its border in a low hedge. It was an ordered land.

'I never noticed that it looked like this,' said Bane.

'It certainly looks better without Dumii armies camped on it,' said Brocando.

'The men under my command were always instructed to treat the country with respect.'

'Others were less respectful.'

'Where are the people?' asked Glurk. 'I'll grant you that a nice baked root goes down well, but all this didn't grow by being whistled at. You're always having to hang about poking at the ground, when you're a farmer.'

There *were* no people. The fruit hung heavy in the bushes along the roadside, but there were none to pick it, except the Munrung children, who did it very well. But there was no-one else.

Snibril took up his spear. This was like hunting. You learned about the different kinds of silence.

There was the silence made by something frightened, in fear of its life. There was the silence made by small creatures, being still. There was the silence made by big creatures, waiting to pounce on small creatures. Sometimes there was the silence made by no-one being there. And there was a very sharp, hot kind of silence made by someone there – *watching*.

Bane had drawn his sword. Snibril thought: soldiers learn about silences, too.

They looked at one another.

'Shall we leave the carts here?' said Snibril.

'Safer to stick together. Don't divide forces unnecessarily. First rule of tactics.'

The carts moved on, slowly, with everyone watching the hairs.

'The bushes just up on the right there,' Bane said, without moving his head.

'I think so, too,' said Snibril.

'They're in there watching us.'

'Just one, I think,' said Snibril.

'I could put a spear into it from here, no trouble,' said Glurk.

'No. We might want to ask it questions afterwards,' said Bane. 'We'll circle around it on either side.'

Snibril crept towards the bush around one side of a hair. He could see it moving slightly. Bane was on the other side of it and Glurk, who could walk very quietly for such a big man, appeared as if by some kind of magic in front of it, with his spear raised.

'Ready?'

'Ready.'

'Yeah.'

Bane took hold of a dust frond, and tugged.

A small child looked up at three trembling blades.

'Um,' it said.

And ten minutes later . . .

A small group of Deftmenes were labouring in the vegetable lines between the hairs. They did not look happy or, for that matter, very well-fed. Several guards were watching them. Even from here, Snibril could see the long snouts.

Among the hairs was Jeopard itself.

It was built on a piece of grit. The actual city was a cluster of buildings at the very top; a spiral roadway wound several times around the grit between the city and the floor. It had a gate at the bottom, but that was just for show. No-one could have got up that road if the people at the top didn't want them to.

There was a movement in the dust, and Glurk crawled up beside Snibril.

'The boy was right. There's mouls and snargs every-where,' he said. 'The whole place is crawling with them.'

64

'They've got the city?' said Snibril.

Glurk nodded. 'That what comes of running around looking for treasure when he ought to have been at home, reigning,' he said, disapprovingly.

'Come on,' said Snibril, 'Let's get back to the camp.'

The carts had been dragged into the undergrowth some way off, and people were on guard.

Pismire, Bane and Brocando were sitting in a semicircle, watching the little boy drinking soup. He had a bottomless capacity for food but, in between mouthfuls, he'd answer Brocando's questions in a very small voice.

'My own brother!' growled Brocando, as the others slipped into the camp. 'But if you can't trust your own family, who can you trust? Turn my back for a few days—'

'A year,' said Bane.

'—and he calls himself king! I never did like Antiroc. Always skulking and muttering and not keen on sports.'

'But how did mouls get into the city?' said Snibril.

'He let them in! Tell the man, Strephon!'

The boy was about seven years old, and looked terrified.

'I . . . I . . . they were . . . everyone fought . . .' he stuttered.

'Come on! Come on! Out with it, lad!'

'I think,' said Bane, 'that perhaps you ought to wander off for a minute or two, perhaps? He might find it easier to talk.'

'I am his *king*!'

'That's what I mean. When they're standing right in front of you, kings are a kind of speech impediment. If you'd just, oh, go and inspect the guard or something . . . ?'

Brocando grumbled about this, but wandered off with Glurk and Snibril.

'Huh. Brothers!' he muttered. 'Nothing but trouble,

65

eh? Plotting and skulking and hanging around and usurping.'

Glurk felt he had to show solidarity with the unofficial association of older brothers.

'Snibril never kept his room tidy, I know that,' he said.

When they got back Strephon was wearing Bane's helmet and looking a lot more cheerful. Bane sent him off with an instruction to do something dangerous.

'If you want it in grown-up language,' he said, 'your brother took over the throne when you didn't come back. He wasn't very popular. There was quite a lot of fighting. So when a pack of mouls arrived one day – he invited them in.'

'He wouldn't!' said Brocando.

'He thought he could hire them as mercenaries, to fight for him. Well, they fought all right. They *say* he's still king, although no-one has seen him. The mouls do all the ruling. A lot of people ran away. The rest are slaves, more or less. Quarrying grit. Forced labour in the fields. That sort of thing.'

'The mouls don't look as if they'd be interested in vegetables,' said Snibril.

'They eat meat.'

Pismire had been sitting against one of the cartwheels, wrapped in the blanket; travel was not agreeing with him. They'd almost forgotten about him.

His words sunk in like rocks. In fact it wasn't the words themselves that were disturbing. Everyone ate meat. But he gave the word a particular edge that suggested, not ordinary meat . . .

Brocando went white.

'Do you mean—?'

'They eat animals,' said Pismire, looking more miserable than Snibril had ever seen him before. 'Unfortunately, they consider everything that's not a moul is an animal. Um. I don't know how to say this

66

. . . do you know what the word "moul" means in moul language? Hmm? It means . . . True Human Beings.'

This sunk in, too.

'We'll attack tonight,' said Brocando. 'No-one's eating *my* subjects.'

'Er,' said Glurk.

'Oh yes,' said Bane. 'Yes, indeed. Fine. Five thousand soldiers couldn't attack Jeopard.'

'That's true,' said Brocando. 'So we—'

'Er,' said Glurk.

'Yes?' said Brocando.

The chieftain appeared to have something on his mind. 'I've heard one or two references just recently to "we",' he said. 'I just want to get this sorted out? No offence. As a reward for rescuing you, we're now going to attack this city that no amount of Dumii soldiers could capture *and* fight a lot of mouls? You want my tribe, which hasn't got a home now, to save your city for you, even though this is impossible? Have I got it right, yes?'

'Good man!' said Brocando, 'I knew we could depend on you! I shall need half a dozen stout-hearted men!'

'I think I can let you have one astonished one,' said Glurk.

'We've got to help,' said Snibril. 'Everyone's too tired to run away. Anyway, what will happen if we don't? Sooner or later we've got to fight these things. It might as well be here.'

'Outnumbered!' said Bane. 'And you're not soldiers!'

'No,' said Glurk. 'We're hunters.'

'Well done!' said Brocando.

Glurk nudged Snibril. 'Have we just volunteered for practically certain death?' he said.

'I think we may have, yes.'

'This kinging is amazing,' said Glurk. 'If we get out of this, I think I'm going to try to learn it.'

*   *   *

Night came. A blue badger, hunting early, nearly blundered into the line of would-be invaders and waddled off hurriedly.

There was a whispered argument going on among the Deftmenes. Some of them wanted to sing as they went into battle, which was a tradition. Brocando kept pointing out that they were going into battle *secretly*, but one or two diehard traditionalists were holding out for the right to sing peaceful songs, which would – they said – totally confuse the enemy. In the end Brocando won by playing the king, and threatening to have everyone who disagreed with him put to death. Glurk was impressed.

When it began to seem to Snibril that the dark Carpet had no ending they reached the road again and, ahead of them, torches burning along its walls, was the city of Jeopard.

Chapter 9

The wights built Jeopard. They brought red wood and sparkling varnish from *achairleg* to pave its streets; from the Hearthlands they led great caravans of the rare jet, to be made into domes and cornices, and cinder and ash for bricks and mortar; at the distant High Gate Land of the Vortgorns they traded their varnish wares for beaten bronze, for doors and pillars; salt and sugar, in great white crystals, were dragged between the hairs by teams of sweating horses, for walls and roofs. And they brought different coloured hairs from all parts of the Carpet. Some became planks and rafters, but most they planted around the city.

Everywhere there were gardens. In the evening light it looked peaceful, but they had to lie low twice when moul cavalry went past on the road.

'In my city, too,' said Brocando.

'You've got a plan, I hope,' said Bane.

'There's another way into the city,' said Brocando.

'I didn't know that.'

'Didn't you?' said Brocando. 'Amazing. All that trouble to built a secret passage and we forgot to tell the Emperor. Remind me to send him a note. Turn right into that little hidden track there.'

'What track?'

Brocando grinned. 'Good, isn't it,' he said.

It looked like an animal path. It wound round and

about the hairs. The dust bushes were much thicker here.

'Planted,' said Brocando.

Eventually, when it was almost dark, they reached a small glade with another ruined temple in it.

'Temples don't last long around here, do they,' said Snibril, looking around at the crowding hairs. Here and there were more statues, half covered in dust.

'This one was built to look ruined,' said Brocando. 'By the wights. For one of my ancestors. The one over there, with the bird's nest on his head and his arm raised—' He hesitated. 'And you're a Dumii, and I've brought you to the secret place,' he said. 'I should have you blindfolded.'

'No,' said Bane. 'You want me to fight for you, then I'm wearing no blindfold.'

'But one day you might come back with an army.'

'I'm sorry you think so,' said Bane stonily.

'As *me*, I don't,' said Brocando. 'As a king, I *have* to think so.'

'Ha!'

'This is stupid,' said Snibril. 'Why bother with a blindfold?'

'It's important,' said Brocando, sulkily.

'You've got to trust one another sooner or later. Who are you going to trust instead? You're men of honour, aren't you?' said Snibril.

'It's not as simple as that,' said Brocando.

'Then make it simple!'

He realized he had shouted. Even Glurk was surprised.

'Well, it's no time to argue,' said Snibril, calming down a bit.

Brocando nodded. 'Yes. Very well. Maybe. I'm sure he's an honourable man. Pull Broc's arm.'

'What?' said Bane.

'Behind you. On the statue. Pull the arm,' said Brocando.

Bane shrugged, and reached for the arm.

'First time a Dumii's ever shaken a Deftmene's hand,' he said. 'I wonder what it'll lead to—'

There was a grinding noise, somewhere under their feet. A slab in the temple floor slid aside, showing a flight of steps.

'It'll lead to the palace,' said Brocando, grinning.

They stared into the square of darkness.

Finally Glurk said: 'You don't mean . . . into the *Underlay*?'

'Yes!'

'But . . . but . . . there's terrible things down there!'

'Just stories for children,' said Brocando. 'Nothing to be frightened of down there.'

He trotted down the steps. Bane went to follow him, and then looked back at the Munrungs.

'What's the matter?' he said.

'Well . . .' said Snibril. What shall I say? Creatures from ancient tales live down there: thunorgs, the horrible delvers, and shadows without number or names. Strange things gnawing at the roots of the Carpet. The souls of the dead. Everything bad. Everything you get . . . frightened by, when you're small.

He looked around at the other tribesmen. They had moved closer together.

He thought: at times like this, we *all* have to forget old things.

'Nothing's the matter,' he said, in what he hoped was a voice full of leadership. 'Come on, lads. Last one in's a—'

'Never mind about the last one,' muttered a voice somewhere towards the back of the group. '*We* want to see what happens to the *first* one.'

Snibril tripped at the bottom of the stairs and landed on a pile of soft dust. Brocando was lighting a torch, taken from a rack of them on one wall of the little

71

cave. One by one the band shuffled down. Brocando moved another lever and the statue trundled back over the hole, leaving them crowded shoulder to shoulder in the red-lit cave.

'All here?' said Brocando, and without waiting for a reply he ducked into a tiny crevice and was gone.

Nearly as bad as discovering all your worst fears are coming true, Snibril thought, is finding out that they're not.

The walls showed up brown in the torchlight, and were covered with tiny hairs that glittered as the light passed them. Sometimes they crossed the entrances to other tunnels. But there were no monsters, no sudden teeth . . .

The path began to slope down and suddenly the light from Brocando's torch dimmed. Snibril started before he realized that they were entering a cavern under the Carpet, with walls so far away that the light was not reflected from them. They passed through many great caverns, the path narrowing and spiralling up around great columns of hair, so that they had to cling to stay on it. Sometimes the light sparkled on a distant wall. While they were edging along one place where the path narrowed almost to nothingness, and cold air rushed up from the depths below, Snibril slipped. Bane, who was next in line, reached out with great presence of mind and grabbed him by the hair just as he was about to totter into the darkness. But the torch slipped from his hands. They peered over the edge to watch it become a spark, then a speck and finally wink out. Something shifted in the dark depths of Underlay, and they heard it scuttle heavily away.

'What was that?' said Snibril.

'Probably a silverfish,' said Brocando. 'They've got teeth bigger than a man, you know. And dozens of legs.'

'I thought you said there was nothing to be afraid of down here!' shouted Glurk.

'Well?', said Brocando, looking surprised. 'Who's afraid of them?'

Anything else in the depths below would hardly have seen them, little specks inching along the roots of the hairs. Eventually Brocando called a halt on the edge of another abyss. There was a narrow bridge stretching across it, and Snibril could just make out a door on the far side.

The king held up the torch and said: 'We are right underneath the rock now.'

The roof of the cavern was gently curved towards its centre, bowed under the great weight above it.

'You are the only people apart from the kings of Jeopard to see this,' Brocando went on. 'After the secret passage was dug, Broc had all the workers personally put to death to stop the secret escaping.'

'Oh? That's part of kinging, too, is it?' said Glurk.

'It used to be,' said Brocando. 'Not any more, of course.'

'Hah!' said Bane.

When they had crossed the bridge Brocando pushed the little wooden door open, revealing a spiral staircase lit by green light filtering down from a tiny circle of light. It was a long climb up the winding staircase, which was so narrow that the boots of the ones in front tangled with the hands of the ones behind, and the torches made flickering shadows of giant warriors against the walls. Ghostly as it was, Snibril welcomed it. He hated the darkness under the Carpet.

Before it reached the circle of green light the stairway opened on to a little landing, just big enough to hold them all. There was another door in the wall.

'Where—' Glurk began.

Brocando shook his head and put his finger to his lips.

There were voices on the other side of the door.

Chapter 10

There were three voices, so loud that they could only be a metre or so from the hidden door.

Snibril tried to imagine faces. One voice was thin and whiny, already raised in complaint.

'Another hundred? But you took fifty only a few days ago!'

'And now we need another hundred,' said a soft voice that made Snibril's hair prickle. 'I advise you to sign this paper, your majesty, and my guards will gather together this hundred and be gone. They will not be slaves. Just . . . assistants.'

'I don't know why you don't just take them,' said the first voice sulkily.

'But you are the *king*,' said the second voice. 'It *must* be right, if the king says so. Everything signed and proper.'

Snibril thought he could hear Bane grinning in the darkness.

'But no-one ever comes back,' said first Voice.

The third voice was like a rumble. 'They like it so much in our lands we just cannot persuade them to return,' it said.

'I don't believe you,' said First Voice.

'That does not really matter,' said Second Voice. 'Sign!'

'No! I will *not*! I am king . . .'

'And you think that I, who made you king, can't . . . *unmake* you?' said Second Voice. 'Your majesty,' it added.

'I'll report you to Jornarileesh! I'll tell on you!' said First Voice, but he did not sound very confident.

'Jornarileesh! You think they care what is done here?' Second Voice purred. 'Sign! Or perhaps Gorash here can find some other use for your hands?'

'Yeah,' said Third Voice. 'A necklace.'

Brocando turned to face the others, while the voices on the other side of the door alternately threatened and whined.

'That's my brother,' he said. 'Such as he is. Here's the plan. We rush in, and we kill as many mouls as possible.'

'You think that's a clever plan?' said Bane.

'Sounds sensible to me,' said Glurk.

'But there's hundreds in the city, aren't there?' said Bane.

'My people will rise up and overthrow them,' hissed Brocando.

'Have they got any weapons, then?' said Bane.

'No, but the mouls have. So they'll start by getting their weapons off them,' said Brocando placidly.

Bane groaned. 'We're all going to die,' he said. 'This isn't tactics. This is just making-it-up-as-you-go-along.'

'Let's start now, then,' said Brocando. He put his foot against the door and pushed. It moved a fraction, and then stopped.

'What's the matter?' said Snibril.

'There's something on the other side,' hissed Brocando. 'There shouldn't be. Everyone give me a hand here.'

They put their shoulders to it. It resisted for a moment, and then flew open. There was a shriek.

For a second the hall was motionless.

Snibril saw a throne lying on the floor. It had blocked the door. Now it lay halfway down the steps and a thin Deftmene was struggling underneath it, making pathetic little noises. Beyond it two mouls were standing, staring at the open doorway. One was big, wide-shouldered, with a pale face almost hidden in his leather helmet. He held a coiled whip in one great paw. Voice Three, Snibril thought. He even *looks* as though he should be called Gorash. Beside him stood a thin moul wearing a long black cloak and a grin like a wolf that's just had dinner. Voice Two, said Snibril to himself. He looks like he ought to have a name with a lot of esses in it – something you can hiss.

Both groups stared at one another for a second.

Then Brocando whirred forward like an enraged chicken, waving his sword. The thin moul leapt backwards and drew its own sword with disheartening swiftness. Gorash uncurled his whip, but found that Bane was suddenly between him and the king.

The Munrungs watched. There seemed to be two ways of swordfighting. Brocando went at it like a windmill, pushing the enemy back by sheer effort. Bane fought quietly, like some kind of machine – stamp, thrust, parry . . . tic toc tic.

'Shouldn't we help?' said Snibril.

'No. Ten to two isn't fair,' said Glurk.

The doors at the end of the throne room burst open and a dozen moul guards ran towards them.

'Oh. This is better, then, is it?' said Snibril.

Glurk threw his spear. One of the guards screamed.

'Yes,' he said.

Snibril found that spears fought well against swords, if you didn't throw them. They could prod, and they could parry. And as more guards poured into the room, he realized that it also helped if you were outnumbered. It made it easier to hit an enemy, for one thing. And since there were so many of them, each one wasn't *too* keen to get involved, taking the view that there was no point in running risks when there were all these other people to do it for them.

This must be how the Deftmenes think, he told himself as he broke a spear over the head of a moul.
Always pick a bigger enemy, because he's easier to
hit . . .

He found himself pressed up against the back of Bane,
who was still fighting in his tictoc way, like someone who
can do it all day.

'I've broken my spear!'

'Use a sword!' said Bane, parrying a thrust from
a desperate guard. 'There's plenty of them on the
floor!'

'But I don't know how to use one!'

'It's easy! The blunt end goes in your hand and the
sharp end goes in the enemy!'

'There must be more to it than that!'

'Yes! Remember which end is which!'

And then it was over. The few remaining guards
fell over one another to get out of the door. Gorash
was dead. The skinny moul dodged a last wild slash
from Brocando's sword and dived through the open
doorway to the secret passage. They heard it running
down the steps.

Snibril looked down at his sword. There was blood
on it, and he hoped it wasn't his.

'Well, that wasn't too hard,' said Glurk.

'There's hundreds more out there,' said Bane, gloomily.

Brocando went to the balcony. Early morning light
was flooding across the hairs. He cupped his hands
around his mouth.

'I'mmm baaaack! Brocandoooo!'

He picked up a dead moul, dragged it to the balcony,
and pushed it over.

There were already some Deftmenes in the square
below the palace. A shout went up.

The king rubbed his hands together.

'Help me with the throne,' he said.

It took three of them to lift it up. Underneath it was Antiroc, who hung limply from Glurk's grip as he was hauled to his feet.

'Give me the crown,' said Brocando, in deadly tones. 'It's the thing on your head. The thing that doesn't belong to you.'

'We thought you were dead—'

'You look overjoyed to see me back,' said Brocando. His expression was terrible.

'Someone had to be king, I had to do my best for the people—'

There was a commotion outside. A moul backed through, with an arrow sticking in it. Half a dozen Deftmenes charged over it. They hardly glanced at Brocando. but bore down with grim determination on Antiroc, who was snatched from Glurk's grasp and hustled towards the balcony.

'You can't let them do that!' said Snibril.

Four Deftmenes had hold of Antiroc's arms and legs, and were swinging him backwards and forwards, high over the roofs of Jeopard. 'A-one-a-two-a-three,' they chanted, the swings getting larger.

'Why not?' said Brocando.

'He's your brother!'

'Hmm? Oh, *all* right. Put him down, people,' said Brocando, 'Come on. Release him. I won't say let him go, you might get the wrong idea. I can't have you subjects throwing my family over the balcony, that would never do.'

'Good,' said Snibril.

'I'll do it myself.'

'No!' It was a chorus. Everyone joined in, especially Antiroc, who joined in even more than everyone else.

'Just joking,' said Brocando, who didn't look it. 'Blast all this . . . beholden to other people. You'll get me feeling guilty for throwing traitors off the rock now. It's a royal tradition. All right, then. He can go.'

Antiroc fell on to his hands and knees. 'You can't do that! They'll kill me!'

'All those people whose relatives you sold to the mouls?' said Brocando. 'Dear me. Of course, you can follow your friend . . .

He waved towards the passage doorway. Antiroc looked horrified.

'But Gormaleesh went down there!' he wailed.

'Was that his name? Right sort of name,' said Brocando. 'You can talk about old times.' He nodded to the four who had been about to de-balcony the usurper. 'If he won't go, give him a helping hand,' he said.

The Deftmenes advanced on Antiroc, murder in their eyes. He looked imploringly at Brocando, hesitated for a moment, and then dashed for the doorway.

It slammed behind him.

'He can kill Gormaleesh or Gormaleesh can kill him, for all I care. Or he can even find his way out,' sighed Brocando. 'But now . . . let's round up the last of the mouls. I shouldn't think they'll put up much of a fight now.'

'What shall we do if we capture them alive, your majesty?' said one of the Deftmenes.

Brocando looked tired. 'Well, we haven't got many dungeons,' he said. 'So perhaps if you can avoid capturing any alive that would help.'

'You mustn't kill an enemy who has thrown down his weapons,' said Bane.

'Can't you? We live and learn. I always thought that was the best time,' said Brocando.

Chapter 11

Snibril sat outside the palace stables, watching Roland investigate the contents of a nosebag. Loose boxes built for the Deftmenes' little six-legged beasts were too small for him, and he had to be tethered in the yard with the carts. He stood there patiently chewing, and made a lighter shadow in the darkness.

Snibril could hear the celebrations going on in the main hall. If he concentrated, he could just hear Pismire playing the fluteharp; it was easy to tell, even with all the other instruments in the Deftmenes' own band, by the way the notes went all over the place without ever hitting the tune. Pismire always said there were some things you should care about enough to do badly.

When Snibril had wandered out Glurk had been delighting everybody by lifting twenty Deftmene children on a bench, and carrying them around the hall. The log fires roared and the plates were emptied and refilled again, and nobody thought of the dark hairs outside, sighing in the night wind, or the little bands of Deftmenes who were hunting down the last of the mouls.

Snibril rubbed his head. It had been aching again, and Pismire's music hadn't helped at all.

He patted Roland absently, and looked out over the city to the deep blue night in the hairs beyond.

'Well, here we are,' said Snibril, 'and can't even remember which direction our old village lies in. Brocando says we can stay here as long as we like. Forever, even. Safe and sound. He says he can always do with a few tall people around the place. But Bane says he's going on to Ware tomorrow, just in case. And my ears hurt.'

It's a big Carpet, he thought. Brocando and Bane are both . . . well, likeable, but they look at the world from opposite ends. Look at the Dumii. Half the time you can see why the Deftmenes don't like them. They're so *fair* about things, in an unimaginative way. And in their unimaginative way, fighting like tictoc men, they built a huge Empire. And Bane hates the idea of kings. But the Deftmenes fight as if they enjoy it, and make up life as they go along, and they'll do anything for their king. You can't expect them to get along with each other—

Roland shifted uneasily. Snibril raised his head, and heard the night breeze die away. The hairs were silent.

He felt a pricking sensation in his feet. The headache was felt like a fire now. The silent Carpet seemed to be waiting . . .

Roland neighed, tugged at his tether. Down in the stables the ponies were kicking their stalls. Dogs barked, down in the city.

Snibril remembered this feeling. But he thought: not here, surely, where it was all so safe?

Yes, he told himself, even here. Fray can be any-where.

He turned and ran up the steps into the palace.

'Fray!' he shouted. In the din, no-one heard. One or two people waved cheerily at him.

He bounded over to the band and snatched a trumpet from one startled Deftmene. He didn't know how to play one, but playing it very badly loudly enough was enough to get something approaching silence.

'Can't you feel it? Fray is coming!' he shouted.

'Coming here?' said Pismire.

'Can't you feel it? Can't you feel it?' Snibril was

desperate with impatience and pain. They were looking at him as if he was mad.

'Get to the carts,' snapped Pismire.

'I can't feel anything,' said Brocando. 'Anyway, Jeopard is safe from any enem—'

Pismire pointed upwards. There were big candle chandeliers hanging from the ceiling. They had begun to swing, very gently.

Kings take some time to grasp an idea, but once they've got a hold they don't let go.

'Run for it! Get everyone outside!' Brocando shouted.

The Munrungs were already streaming through the door. Tables were overturned as people scurried from the hall, grabbing their children as they ran. Pismire caught hold of a pillar to steady himself as they jostled past, and yelled above the noise: 'The ponies! Harness them to the carts!'

The lamps were swinging quite noticeably now. A jug bounced off a table and shattered on the floor. A couple of candles teetered out of the crazily-weaving lamps.

There was a far-off thump. The whole rock shook.

The heavy lintel over the door shivered and sagged. Glurk strode forward among the bewildered throng and put his shoulders under it, and stood with one hand braced against each doorpost while people scrambled under his arms and between his legs.

Snibril was already leading the screaming ponies out of their stable. No sooner was each cart moving than it was loaded down with people. And still people were coming, scurrying along under treasured possessions and small children. The hall was already blazing.

He lifted four Deftmenes on to Roland's back and sent the horse after the carts, then struggled through the flow to the hall. Glurk had been forced almost to his knees, his face purple, the veins throbbing in his neck.

Snibril grabbed an arm. 'Come on! The whole building is going to go!'

'No,' came the low growl, 'Pismire and the others are still in there.'

Another tremor shook the hall. A pillar cracked, and Glurk grunted. 'Get out of the way!' came a whisper from deep in his throat, 'it's going to go.'

The rock shook underfoot.

'I'll . . . I'll get some people with beams and things!' said Snibril. 'We'll soon have you out! Don't go away!'

Glurk grunted as Snibril hurried away.

Pismire appeared through the smoke, a scrap of his robe tied over his face, shepherding some bewildered revellers in front of him. He pushed them out under Glurk's arm.

'What are you doing, still here?' he said.

'Goin' to be in a story,'said Glurk

Bane groped his way out of the billows, a rag pressed over his mouth. 'Come on,' he said, 'Brocando's got the secret door open.'

'Help me with this idiot,' said Pismire.

'Looks wedged to me,' said Bane.

'Gonna be a hero,' said Glurk.

'Shut up,' said Pismire. 'That's what comes of listening to stories on an empty head. Stupid idea, anyway, wedging yourself under the door like that . . .'

Glurk turned his head with difficulty.

'What?' he said.

'Boneheaded, I call it,' said Pismire. The ceiling at the end of the hall collapsed.

'Why, you daft . . . old . . .' Glurk began. He rose on one knee, then on both, then slowly raised the beam above his head. Then he stepped forward and waved a finger under Pismire's nose.

'I saved a lot—' he began. Then he toppled over.

'Right, it worked. Grab him,' said Pismire. 'That wall's falling in.'

They took an arm each, and stumbled out of the way as the lintel thudded into the floor, splitting it. Pismire squinted at the roof.

'Quickly!'

Brocando was standing by the door to the stairway.

'Come on!'

Glurk started to cough. Pismire pushed a rag into his hand.

'Put it over your mouth and nose,' he said. 'Damp cloth. Helps with the smoke. Important safety information.'

'Tastes of wine,' said Glurk thickly, as they half-pushed, half-carried him through the doorway.

'Only thing there was,' said Pismire. 'Now . . . down!'

The whole roof fell in.

They ran down the steps, the others carrying Glurk between them like a battering ram. The roaring died away and all that could be heard was the thudding of their feet on the stone.

'Not out of the hairs yet!' panted Brocando.

'What . . . mean?' puffed Pismire.

'No torches!'

Pismire only had enough breath left to grunt.

'!'

They piled into the little door at the bottom of the steps, and lay panting in the blackness.

'Well, there's no going back up,' came Brocando's voice. 'The door's under a mound of rubble now.'

'Do you think you can find the way to the statue in the dark?' said Bane.

'That was the first time I've ever been down here!' wailed Brocando.

'But there must be other entrances,' said Pismire.

He thought of the deep crevasses and windy caves of Underlay, and the stories of the creatures that dwelt there. Of course, he didn't believe in them. He'd *told* them, because the handing on of an oral mythology was very important to a developing culture, but he didn't *believe* in supernatural monsters. He shivered. He hoped they didn't believe in him.

In the darkness he heard the creak of the door.

'If we keep together and test every step, we should be safe,' came Brocando's unsteady voice. 'There's four of us. What would dare attack us?'

'Lots of things.'

'Apart from them.'

Glurk got heavier and heavier as the hours passed. They edged him along narrow paths in the dark, and dragged him through what felt, to judge by the change in the air, to be large caves. They carried him head first and feet first, sometimes propping him up against a hair root while they inched hand in hand along strange paths. They scrambled among thick roots and crept around holes so deep that a warm wind rushed up from them.

Eventually they sat down for a rest. They were walking endlessly. It wasn't as if they were getting anywhere.

'What's below Underlay?' said Brocando.

'The Floor,' said Pismire's voice, out of the darkness.

'What's below that?'

'Nothing. Something has to be below everything else. That's the Floor. That's as far as there is. You might as well ask what's above the Carpet.'

'Well, what *is* above the—'

'How should I know? We've got far too many problems down here right now to worry about what's up there.'

'The Carpet can't go on forever, though.'

'It goes on far enough for me!' said Pismire testily.

Brocando felt the air move in front of his face. It was strange, talking to people when everything was completely black. For all he knew, they could be sitting right on the edge of another hole. Everything had to be done by feel.

'Pismire?' he said.

'What now?'

'What about mouls? Do they come down here?'

'It's your tunnel. You should know. I can't imagine why they'd want to, though. I shouldn't think they'd like it any more than we do.'

'Correct.'

There was silence.

'Was that you?'

'I thought it was you.'

'Brocando?'

'Pismire?'

'Bane?'

'What?'

'You see,' said Gormaleesh's voice by Pismire's ear, 'we can see in the dark.'

They didn't fight. How could you, when you might as easily hit a friend as an enemy?

It was the darkness that was the worst bit. And then the claws that gripped them, as easily as a child grips a toy.

'Well, well,' said Gormaleesh, from somewhere nearby. 'What an unexpected treat.'

'Is my brother with you?' said Brocando.

After a pause, Gormaleesh said, 'In a manner of speaking. Now, you will do what I say. The little king will hold on to Purgish's tail. The old man hold on to the king's belt. The Dumii soldier hold on to the old man's belt. Anyone let go, anyone try to run away, that person is a dead person.'

Brocando, who could count quite quickly for a king, said, 'But what about– ow!'

'Sorry,' said Pismire, who could count faster, 'Did

I accidentally kick you? Well, he's right. He's got *all three* of us.'

'But we can't leave Gl— ow! Oh. Yes. Of course. Yes, I *see*. You're right.' Brocando's voice suddenly took on the kind of excited conspiratorial tone that would have made anyone smell a rat who didn't already smell like a moul. '*All three* of us. Yes. You've definitely got *all three* of us. How *well* can you see in the dark, incidentally? Probably not one-hundred-per-cent, eh?'

Oh, no, Pismire thought. How can they not get suspicious after that?

'Ow!' said Gormaleesh.

'Moul scum,' said Bane. 'When I get out I'll—'

There was the sound of a slap in the darkness.

'When you get out,' said Gormaleesh, 'you will do exactly as I say. Bring them along.'

Well done, thought Pismire. Bane can count fast as well.

They were marched in shuffling single file for quite a short time. They must have been close to a way up to the surface. Pismire felt his hands guided to a ladder. We're going up and out, he thought. If Glurk wakes up, how will he know?

He climbed a few steps, and then let himself drop again.

'Ow! My leg! Ow!' The noise echoed around the caves of Underlay.

'What is the matter with your leg, old man?' said Gormaleesh.

'Nothing,' said Pismire, and climbed back up the ladder.

And if Glurk hasn't heard that, we're done for.

It was already night on the surface.

They'd climbed out into a clearing, a long way from Jeopard. It seemed to be a gathering place for the

87

surviving mouls from the city. The prisoners were tied up with leather thongs and thrown down by a bush. Nearby, a pack of snargs eyed them hungrily.

The mouls were talking in their own language, occasionally turning to look at the prisoners.

'Can you understand them?' said Pismire.

'Very crudely,' said Bane. 'They're taking us somewhere. Called . . . *gargatass*, if that means anything.'

'That's their word for the High Gate Land, I think,' said Pismire. 'Where the Vortgorns live.'

'Them? They're our mortal enemies,' said Brocando.

'I thought the Dumii were your mortal enemies,' said Pismire.

'We like to have several mortal enemies at one time,' said Brocando. 'Just in case we run out.'

Pismire took no notice. He was lying a little apart from the other two, and could see behind the snarg pack. In the glow of the moul's campfire he could just make out a guard lounging by the little overgrown entrance to Underlay, with his snarg tethered to a dust bush.

An arm was slowly growing out of the bush behind the unsuspecting moul. It stopped a few inches above his head, and carefully removed his helmet. The moul turned, and met a fist coming the other way. The arm caught him before he fell and dragged him into the bush . . .

A moment later the hand appeared by the snarg, and started untethering it. It looked up, and with horror Pismire saw its eyes narrow. Before it could growl, though, the hand bunched up into a knotted fist and smacked it smartly between the eyes. He heard the creature give a little sigh, and saw it fall over slowly. Before it reached the ground the tether tightened and tugged it into the bush.

Pismire didn't know why, but he felt sure that everything was going to be all right.

Or, at least, more all right than it was now.

Chapter 12

All that night they journeyed south. Most of the pack were mounted on their snargs, though the prisoners and their guards had to run along in the middle of the jostling bodies. Dawn came. The hairs around had changed from deep purple to red again.

The next days merged for the prisoners into one continuous blur of running feet and moul voices. The hairs changed from crimson to orange, from orange to black. Feet blistered and bled, and minds were muddled by the constant pounding. Twice they crossed white Dumii roads, late at night, when no-one was abroad, and passed by sleeping villages like shadows.

And then there was a place . . . above the Carpet.

The hairs were bent almost double under the weight of the High Gate Land of the Vortgorns. First it was a glimmer between the hairs. An hour later it loomed above them, the largest thing Pismire had ever seen. He had read about it, back in the old days, but the descriptions in the books had not got it right at all. You needed bigger words than 'big'.

It looked the largest thing there could ever be. The Carpet was big, but the Carpet was . . . everything. It didn't count. It was too big to have a size. But the High Gate Land was small enough to be really huge.

It looked quite near even from a long way off. And it shone.

It was bronze. All the metal in the Carpet came from there. Snibril knew that much. The Vortgorns had to trade it with the wights for food. Nothing grew on the High Gate Land.

'*On Epen Ny*,' said Pismire, under his breath, while the party stopped for a brief rest under the very walls of the Land. Brocando had immediately fallen asleep. He had shorter legs than everyone else.

'What?' said Brocando, waking up.

'That's the battle cry of the Vortgorns,' said Pismire. 'Lots of people remembered it, but not for very long. It was often the last thing they heard. *On Epen Ny*. It's written on the Land. Huge metal letters. I've seen pictures. It'd take you all day just to walk around one letter.'

'Who wrote them?' said Brocando, eyeing the guards.

'The Vortgorns think it was done by Fray,' said Pismire. 'Superstition, of course. There's probably some natural explanation. The Vortgorns used to say there's letters *under* the Land, too. They dug tunnels and found them. Some of them say . . .' he concentrated '. . . I ZABETH II. The Vortgorns seem to think that's very important.'

'Giant letters can't just grow by themselves,' said Brocando.

'They might. Who knows?'

They looked up at the Land. Around the base of it ran a road. It was wider than a Dumii road, yet in the shadow of that looming wall it looked thinner than a thread.

'Anyone know much about the Vortgorns?' said Pismire. 'I've read about them, but I don't remember ever seeing one.'

'Like the Dumii, but without their well-known flair and excitement,' said Brocando.

'Thank you,' said Bane gravely.

'Well, living on metal all the time must give you a very sombre and mystical view of life,' said Pismire.

'Whose side are they on?' said Brocando.

'Sides? Their own, I suppose, just like everyone else.'

The mouls milled around aimlessly, waiting for something.

'I suppose we're waiting to get up there,' said Brocando, 'but how?'

'Dumii patrols have been all round the Land and found no way in,' said Bane.

Pismire, who was squinting upwards, said: 'Ah. But I think this remarkable mechanism is the secret.'

High above them was a speck on the wall. Slowly it grew bigger, became a wide platform sliding down the bronze. They could see heads peering over the side of it.

When it landed beside the pack Pismire saw that it was a simple square made of hair planks with a railing around them. Four bronze chains, one from each corner, rose up into the mists. A man stood at each corner. Each one was as tall as Bane. They wore helmets and body armour of beaten bronze, and carried by their sides long bronze swords. Their shields were bronze, round like the High Gate Land itself, and their hair was the colour of the metal. They had short square beards, and grey eyes that stared calmly ahead of them. Too much metal, Pismire thought. It enters the soul.

'Er,' Brocando whispered, as they were pushed forward on to the platform, 'you haven't, er, seen or heard anyone, as it were, following us? Someone, such as it might be, your chief? The big fellow?'

'Not a sign since we left Underlay,' said Pismire. 'I've been watching and listening very carefully.'

'Oh, dear.'

'Oh, no. That's good news. It means he's out there somewhere. If I had seen or heard anything, I'd know it wasn't Glurk. He's a *hunter*, you see.'

91

'Good point. Ow!' A whip stung Brocando's legs as the mouls led their nervous mounts on to the planks.

When the last one was aboard one of the bronze guards took a trumpet from his belt and blew one note. The chains around them shook and rattled as they took up the slack and then, with a creaking, the platform swung off the ground and up towards the Land.

Pismire had been forced up against one of the railings by the press of animals, and so it was that he saw a shadow detach itself from the dust bush by the base of the wall and dash for the rising platform, trying to find a handhold on the underside.

He saw it leap; but at that moment the platform swung, and he could not see the shadow again.

Up rose the entrance to the Land, through swirling fogs, and then he realized he was looking out *over* the Carpet. Beneath him the tips of the hairs gleamed in the mist. It made him dizzy, so he tried to take his mind off things by giving the others a short lecture.

'The Deftmenes say that this Land fell out of the above many years ago. The Vortgorns were just another small tribe that lived nearby. They climbed it, too, and hardly ever come down.'

'Then why are mouls in the Land?'

'I'd rather not think about it,' said Pismire. 'The Vortgorns may be a bit dull, but I've never understood them to be evil.'

The platform ground on up the wall until, suddenly, it stopped. Before them was a bronze gate, built on top of the wall. Just above it heavy gantries carried the pulleys that raised and lowered the platform. They were plated with bronze, and studded with spikes. The gateway was spiked, and the portcullis in it was tipped with more spikes. Beneath them, far beneath, lay the Carpet.

'They like their privacy, these people,' remarked Bane.

Behind him Gormaleesh hissed. 'Look your last at your precious Carpet. You will not see it again.'

'Ah. Melodrama,' said Pismire.

'So you think—' Gormaleesh began.

The last word ended on a yelp. Brocando had sunk his teeth into the moul's leg.

Whimpering with pain and rage Gormaleesh picked up the Deftmene king and rushed with him to the edge of the platform, raising him over his head.

Then he lowered his arms, and smiled. 'No,' he said slowly. 'No. Why? Soon you will wish that I had thrown you over. Throwing you over now would be mercy. And I don't feel merciful . . .'

He dropped the trembling Brocando by the others just as the portcullis rose.

'I wasn't shaking,' said Brocando. 'It's just a bit chilly up here.'

The mouls marched on to the High Gate Land. Pismire saw a broad metal plateau, with what looked like hills in the distance. On either side as they marched were cages, with thick bars. They contained snargs. There were small brown snargs from the Woodwall lands, red snargs from the west, and black snargs with overlong teeth. Whatever their colour, they all had one thought in mind. They hurled themselves at their bars as the prisoners passed.

On they went, and there were compounds where snargs were being broken in and trained. Further, and there were more cages, bigger than those of the snargs. They contained . . . strange creatures.

They were huge. They had fat barrel bodies with ridiculous small wings, and long thin necks tipped with heads that wobbled slowly round as they passed. At the other end they had a stubby little tail. Their legs didn't look thick enough to support them. Oh, they were thick – but something that big ought to have legs as thick as giant hairs.

One of the creatures poked its head through the bars and looked down at Pismire. Its eyes were large but bright and oddly intelligent, and topped by enormous bushy brows.

'A pone,' he said. 'A pone! From the utter east, where the very fringes of the Carpet touch the Floor. The biggest things in the Carpet. Oh, if we had a few of those at our command—'

'I think perhaps they are under the command of the mouls,' said Bane.

The pone watched him pass.

They reached the angular metal hills and went through a dark archway. Inside they were handed over to other, swarthier, mouls.

There was a maze of tunnels that echoed with the chip-chip of hammers, but these they passed, going deeper, until they came to a dimly-lit hall lined with doors. One was opened, and they were thrown inside.

As they struggled on the dank floor Gormaleesh's grinning face appeared at the bars, lit red in the torchlight of the dungeons. 'Enjoy the hospitality of our dungeons while you may. Soon you'll go to the mines. There you will not sleep. But you'll be safe from Fray!'

'Why do they talk like that?' said Pismire. 'Melodrama. I'm amazed he doesn't go "harharhar".'

'Gormaleesh!' said Bane.

The moul reappeared. 'Yes, lowly scum?' he said.

'Lowly scum,' said Pismire. 'Imagination of a loaf of bread, that one.'

'When we get out of here I'm going to find you and kill you,' said Bane, in quite normal conversational tones. 'I thought I ought to tell you now. I wouldn't want you to say afterwards that you hadn't been warned.'

Gormaleesh stepped back, and then said, 'Your threats I treat with scorn. Harharhar!'

Pismire nodded happily. 'Knew he would, sooner or later,' he said to himself.

They lay in the darkness, listening to the distant knocking of the hammers.

'So these are the mines,' said Brocando, 'where my people have been taken. Mining metal.'

'Everyone's people, by the sound of it,' said Pismire.

He lay staring at the dark, wondering about Glurk. He could have imagined the shadow. And Snibril . . . well, perhaps he *did* get out before the roof fell in . . .

They were roughly woken by the prodding of a spear.

Two mouls were standing in the doorway, grinning down at them. 'These three for the mines, eh?'

'Aye,' came a growl from outside. Pismire's ears pricked.

'That one's a bit small, and that one's an old codger. Still, use up the old ones first, eh?'

'Let's see 'em,' came the voice from outside.

The prisoners were dragged upright, and had their thongs inspected before they were thrust out into the dim hall. A bronze-clad Vortgorn stood there, terrible in the half-light.

'You stupid oafs,' he snarled at the mouls. 'Look at their bonds! Practically falling off!' And he strode forward and caught up Pismire's hands. The old man looked for a moment into familiar brown eyes, one of which winked at him.

'We tightened them special!' said one moul indignantly.

'Oh yes? Look at this one, then.'

The two mouls slunk over and stood one on either side of the Vortgorn.

One said: 'They're as tight as a . . .'

The Vortgorn reached out and placed one gnarled hand about each hairy neck. The voice faded into a strangled squeak. The Vortgorn brought his hands together with a satisfying crack, and let the stunned creatures drop.

Glurk removed his helmet.

'Well, here we are, then,' he said.

He couldn't resist dancing a little jig in front of their staring faces. Then he put his helmet back on again.

'We left you in Underlay!'

'How d'you come here?'

'Was it you I saw?' asked Pismire. 'It was, wasn't it?'

'Safety first, stories later,' said Glurk.

He took a knife from his belt and cut their ropes. They rubbed some life into their numb wrists while he dragged the guards into the cell and locked them in, despite Brocando pointing out that the best time to kill an enemy was when they were unconscious.

Glurk came back with their swords. 'They're nasty things, but better than nothing if it comes to a fight,' he said. 'Try to look like prisoners if anyone sees you. There's all sorts up here. You might not be noticed.'

Glurk led, in his Vortgorn armour. Twice they met moul guards who paid no attention to him until it was too late.

'Where are we going?' said Pismire.

'I've found some friends.'

'We ought to rescue the prisoners,' said Brocando.

'There's thousands of them. Thousands of mouls, too,' said Glurk. 'Too many.'

'That's right,' said Bane. 'We've got to get out. Then we can get help. And *don't* say that if they've got a lot of Deftmenes prisoner it means we've got an army right inside their lines.'

'I've seen some of the prisoners, too,' said Glurk. 'They ain't in any condition to fight, if you want my opinion.'

'You're talking about Deftmenes, you know,' said Brocando stoutly.

Glurk peered around a corner, and then beckoned them to follow him. 'I know,' he said. 'And it's still

96

true. What I'm saying is, it's not a case of stealing a bunch of keys and unlocking a few doors and shouting, "Harharhar, my people, throw off your shackles". This is *real*. And I've been *listening*. You know why the mouls attacked Jeopard?'

'To subjugate and enslave a proud people,' said Brocando.

'For grit.'

'*Grit?*'

'That's what Jeopard's built on, isn't it? Stone chisels, see. They use dozens of 'em just to hack out a bit of metal.'

'My lovely city—'

'Grit,' said Glurk.

'My palace—'

'Grit, too.'

'Metal,' said Bane. 'They're trying to get as much metal as they can. Metal weapons'll beat varnish and wood any day.'

'Why all this effort, I wonder?' said Pismire.

'Ware's only a few days away,' said Bane. '*That's* why. We've got to warn people.'

'Come on. In here,' said Glurk.

'Here' was a long cave mined out of the bronze. Light filtered in from holes in the ceiling, showing dim shadows lining the walls. The air was warm and smelt of animal. The prisoners heard the shifting of great feet in their stalls, and deep breathing. There was a movement, and a pair of green eyes came towards them in the semi-darkness.

'What's your business here?' said the moul guard.

'Ah,' said Glurk, 'I have brought the prisoners! Harharhar!'

The guard looked suspiciously at the four of them. 'What for?' it said.

Glurk blinked at him.

'Enough of this talking, harharhar,' he said eventually, and hit the guard on the head.

The green eyes went out.

'I runs out of ideas after a while,' said Glurk,

Pismire's eyes had grown accustomed to the gloom. It was a big cave, but it didn't look as big as it really ought to have done because of the enormous size of the things in it.

'These are pones, aren't they?' said Brocando.

'Not easy to mistake for anything else. Why are they here?' said Pismire.

'They turns the wheels for the lifting platform,' said Glurk. 'They're used for all the heavy work. Know something? They're intelligent.'

'No, that's just a story,' said Pismire airily. 'They *look* bright, I'll grant you, but the head's tiny compared to the body. They've got a brain the size of a dried pea.'

'But a very *clever* dried pea,' said Glurk. 'I lay low in here last night. They've got a language. All made up of thumps and nose honks. Watch.'

A tiny head was lowered towards him out of the shadows, and two bright eyes blinked.

'Er . . . if you can understand me, stamp twice,' he said hoarsely.

Thud. Thud.

Even Glurk himself looked surprised.

'These are friends. You'll help, OK?'

Thud. Thud.

'That means yes,' said Glurk.

'Really?' said Pismire.

'There's his saddle, by the stall.'

It was more like a small castle. It had wide girths made of red cloth studded with bronze, and a roof over it, hung with curtains and bells. Inside were cushioned seats, and on the decorated harness was the word 'Acretongue' in tarnished bronze letters.

Pismire sidled closer to the pone while the others were manhandling the saddle, and held up his hand with the fingers spread out.

'How many fingers am I holding up?' he said suspiciously.

Thud. Thud. Thud. Thud.

'Aha! So much for—'

Thud.

'Lucky guess.'

The pone lumbered down on to his knees to let them heave the saddle on to his back.

Then he opened his mouth and trumpeted.

It sounded like the creaking of a door, magnified a thousand times – but it waved and changed as well, and seemed to contain a lot of busy little other sounds. Language, thought Pismire. Language without words, but still language.

I wonder if the wights invented that, too? People used to have language without words. We still have. We say 'Hmm?' and 'Uh' and 'Arrgh!', don't we?

What am I thinking? These are *animals*.

Just very bright ones, perhaps. Very bright indeed.

The other pones raised their heads and answered, with a variety of blasts and trills. Glurk motioned the others up on to Acretongue's back.

'The mouls will have heard that,' said Pismire.

'Won't matter,' said Glurk. 'The pones have decided to go home.'

'You mean they could have gone any time?' said Brocando, watching the huge animals leaving their stalls in an orderly line.

'They *liked* it here when the Vortgorns ran the place,' said Glurk. 'They likes stuff they find interesting. The mouls don't interest them any more. They don't like them. I think they think we're interesting.'

'Now listen, Glurk,' said Pismire, 'I mean, I'm not

saying you're not, you know, quite bright, but I don't think you could have learned a language and all these other things in just a few—'

'Didn't,' said Glurk, smirking. 'Knew what to expect before I come here.'

'How—'

'Enough of this talking, harharhar,' said Glurk. 'Tell you later. Be polite, by the way. She said they understand people very well.'

'Don't believe it,' said Pismire.

One of the pones blew a raspberry in his ear.

'That means they think you're interesting,' said Glurk.

'And who's *she*?' Pimsire demanded.

'Tell you soon,' said Glurk. He was enjoying himself in a quiet way. For the whole of his life Pismire had known more than he did. It was nice, just for once, to be Mr Answers.

At the far end of the cave was a thick bronze door. The first two pones walked straight into it, tearing it off its hinges. Once outside the herd broke into a trot, with Acretongue moving up into the lead.

On his trumpeted signal, it became a gallop. It looked ponderous and funny, until you realized that those great big bouncing balls would walk through a house without noticing it.

Up on Acretongue's back the four of them were shaken like small peas in a big pot. Pismire saw a pack of mounted mouls galloping after them, spears ready to throw. Acretongue must have seen them too, because he bellowed like a distressed trumpet.

Three pones detached themselves from the herd and turned. The mouls suddenly realized that they weren't chasing a herd of fleeing animals . . .

Pismire stood up in the saddle. 'They've gone over them!' he said.

'What, do you mean they jumped?' asked Brocando.

'No! I mean just . . . over.'

'They hate mouls,' said Glurk. 'Hate 'em more than any other creatures do. They think they're very uninteresting.'

Ahead of them was the archway, surrounded by a milling throng of mouls and Vortgorns. 'But all they've got to do is lower that platform and we're done for,' shouted Pismire.

'They won't,' yelled Glurk, and pointed. *'He* powers the platform!'

Beside the gateway they noticed for the first time a large treadmill. There was a pone in it. A pack of mouls were attacking it with whips and goads. But it stood stolidly, trumpeting. Acretongue bellowed back.

'They'll rescue it,' said Glurk. 'By the way – er, what was it – oh, yeah, they hate sharp things even more than mouls, so we got to be careful with spears and things . . .'

Some pones hurled themselves towards the mill, tossing mouls aside like dust. Their heavy jaws snapped through the bars. The caged pone shrugged itself free, paused for a moment to stamp on a couple of mouls who had been poking it the hardest, and then leapt through the gateway.

'They must be mad!' said Pismire. 'That platform won't hold them!'

'We shall see,' said Glurk, as they clattered on to it. The other pones piled on behind them, and Pismire noticed that, though they went out of their way to trample on mouls, they avoided the running Vortgorns. Vortgorns were still a bit interesting.

He expected the platform to split under the weight of the pones. It didn't – quite – but something went clang above them and the remains of the treadmill spun until it was nothing but a blur. The chains shrieked over their pulleys. The wall rushed past. Only Glurk sat calmly.

101

Even Pismire had crouched down in the saddle. They were going to be crushed when they hit the bottom, he knew. Brocando hung on and moaned, with his eyes shut. Even Bane had slumped down, bracing himself for the shock.

So only Glurk saw the pones leaping from the platform, one by one.

The tiny wings opened. They were too small to carry pones – but they worked. They whirled madly and the pones stayed up, drifting gently between the hairs.

With only Acretongue's weight upon it the platform slowed down, and hit the dust with a thud. Acretongue lumbered off, while all about them pones crashed down through the hairs like falling fruit.

The others looked up at Glurk's face.

'You knew we wouldn't crash!' said Pismire accusingly.

'*Hoped*,' said Glurk. 'I wasn't too sure, even after all Culaina said.'

'Who's Culaina? Is he the *she*?' said Pismire. He was badly rattled. He was kind enough in his way, but knowing more than Glurk about almost everything was one of the few things he was sure he was good at. He wasn't used to this.

Another pone bounced on to the dust beside them. They're lighter than they look, he thought. Balloons with wings. No wonder they don't like sharp objects . . .

'Culaina's hard to describe,' said Glurk. 'I think she's a sort of wight.'

'A *sort* of wight?' said Pismire.

'You'll have to ask her yourself,' said Glurk. 'We're going to see her now.' Acretongue's head dipped, and he began to plod between the hairs.

'No, we're not,' said Bane. 'We must go to Ware!'

'Back to Jeopard, you mean!'

'Ware's only a few days away. I have to tell them about this!'

'They might know already,' said Pismire, glumly.

'They don't,' said Glurk.

'How do you know?'

'We're the only ones who know about the moul army,' said Glurk. 'We'll have to go to Ware to warn people. But first we've *got* to go back to talk to Culaina.'

'This wight? Why?' said Pismire.

'To tell her what we've seen,' said Glurk, smiling in a puzzled kind of way. He scratched his head. 'So she can remember what we tell her now and tell me two days ago. When I met her.'

Brocando opened his mouth, but Pismire waved him into silence.

'Wights remember the future as well as the past,' he said. 'But . . . look, they never *tell* anyone, Glurk.'

'This one does,' said Glurk. 'Don't look at me like that. You think I could make this sort of thing *up*?'

Chapter 13

'Following you was easy enough,' said Glurk. 'I mean, twenty people leave a trail, no problem there. Half the time I had to be careful I didn't walk into you. And then I thought . . . they're going south in a straight line, so I might as well go on ahead, spy out the land, see what's happening. One person can move a lot faster than twenty, so why not? I'd got a snarg to ride, too. They respond well to a bit of kindness,' he said. 'Mind you, you have to use quite a lot of cruelty as well. And that's how I met Culaina. She's very strange.'

There was a pause. Then Pismire said, 'I think we missed something there.'

'You'll see where she lives,' said Glurk. 'I . . . er . . . I don't think people see it unless she wants 'em to. *I've* never seen anything like it. And there she was and . . . and . . . she told me where you were going, and how I could hang on to the bottom of that lifting cart, and pinch the armour off a Vortgorn, and release the pones, and how they could fly . . . everything.'

'How did she know all this?' Brocando demanded.

'Because we're going to tell her,' said Glurk. 'Don't ask me how it works.'

'They remember forwards as well as backwards,' said Bane.

'But they must never tell!' said Pismire. 'Otherwise dreadful things could happen!'

'I don't know about that,' said Glurk, guardedly. 'The way I see it, you've been freed . . . that doesn't sound dreadful.'

'But we must get back to the tribe,' said Pismire.

'And my people!' said Brocando. 'They need us!'

'I've been thinking about that,' said Glurk. 'There's two hundred Munrungs and three thousand Deftmenes, and they're all armed and together and . . . they need *us*? We've got some good lads in the tribe. And Snibril's with them . . . isn't he?'

'Er,' said Brocando. 'Yes. We hope so.'

'Right, then. And your people know how to fight. We're four people in a strange land with enemies all over the place . . . I think we need *them*. Anyway, we must see Culaina.'

'But she's told you, and it worked,' said Brocando. 'We can say thank you some other time—'

'No,' said Pismire. 'If Glurk's right, and she's told him something she remembers from the future, and we *don't* go . . . then, I don't know, anything could happen. The whole fabric of the Carpet could roll up, or something. It would be the worst thing that could ever happen anywhere.'

'Worse than—?' Brocando began.

'Worse than anything you could possibly imagine,' said Pismire.

'That's what she said you'd say,' said Glurk.

They all thought about this.

'She must trust you a lot, then,' said Bane.

For the rest of that day the pones moved on. On Acretongue's back the four dozed, or looked out silently at the lengthening shadows. But for most of the time they were each busy with their own thoughts.

Dust grew luxuriantly underfoot, and in it unseen little creatures buzzed and clicked. And growing on the apple-green fluff that draped itself in thick festoons high above were flowers, fluff flowers, bigger than a man, with petals that glittered in a thousand shades of green from deep olive to cool yellow, that gave out a scent that filled the glades and tasted like the colour of green.

'Now this is very interesting,' began Pismire, sitting up. It was the first time any of them had spoken in an hour.

He stopped, and stared across the clearing. Every pone turned its head in that direction.

'It's something you don't often see,' he added. The others looked where he pointed.

Among the greenery at the far side of the glade a wild pig was watching them solemnly. As they all turned it backed away hastily, and they could hear it crashing off through the hairs.

'That's common enough,' grunted Bane.

'It's just that it was brown,' said Pismire, 'it should have been green. Almost all wild creatures in the Carpet take on the colour of the hairs where they were born. Protective camouflage.'

'Perhaps it just wandered here,' said Bane.

'No,' said Glurk, grinning. 'Something brought it here. We're nearly there. You'll be amazed. You really will.'

The pones turned, and pushed their way along another track. As they shouldered their way through the thick fronds scores of small creatures scurried away hurriedly. They were all the colours of the Carpet.

And then the pones stepped through . . .

Hairs clustered in closely on the borders of a wide clearing, reflecting the dim glow from the thing in its centre.

It was one uncut crystal of sugar. High as the Great Palace of Jeopard, whiter than a bone, the crystal glittered coldly in the green dimness. It caught all the light that filtered through the densely packed dust, and within its marvellous cubic bulk a shifting white glow danced. In parts it shone like polished varnish, reflecting the faces of the creatures that clustered round it.

There were dust rabbits and weft borers of all colours, pigs by the herd, long-necked soraths, patient fat tromps, gromepipers, scurrying goats with spiral horns and creatures even Pismire could not recognize: a scaly thing with spikes on its back, and a long creature that seemed to be all legs. The clearing was filled with the sound of a thousand tongues . . . licking.

Acretongue and his herd pounded forward, almost throwing Glurk and the rest out of the saddle. Smaller creatures leapt aside hastily to give them room.

'It's . . . beautiful,' whispered Brocando at last. Bane stood staring up, gaping. Even Pismire was impressed.

They climbed down from the pone's back and walked gingerly up to the smooth surface. The animals licking the sugar hardly paid them any attention.

Glurk cracked a piece off with his knife, and stood crunching it thoughtfully. 'Have a taste,' he said, tossing a piece to Bane. Bane bit it cautiously.

'Sugar,' said Bane. 'I've only ever tasted it once before. There was a crystal down near the Hearthlands. The Emperor used to get it in very small amounts.'

'Like honey, but different,' said Brocando. 'How does it get here?'

'Like Grit, and Salt, and Ash do. From above,' said Pismire. 'We don't know any more than that.'

Instinctively they looked up at the spreading hairs.

'Well, here's our lunch, anyway,' Brocando's voice broke the silence. 'Take your pick – fried tromp or baked gromer. No wonder they're all colours. This must attract them from everywhere. Mind you,' he added, 'it hardly seems sporting to kill them while they're not looking.'

'So put away your knife,' said a new voice.

Pismire choked on his sugar.

A figure stood a little way away. It was tall, with the

thin face of a wight, and looked ghostly in the light of the crystal. It had a mass of white hair – it was hard to see where the hair ended and the shapeless long robe began. And she was young, but as she moved sometimes she was old, and sometimes she was middle-aged. Time moved across her face like shadows.

One of her hands held the collar of a white snarg, which was swishing its tail menacingly.

'Um,' said Glurk, 'this is Culaina.'

The wight walked past them and patted Acretongue's flank. The pone's long neck turned and his little eyes looked at Culaina; then he clumsily lowered himself to his knees and laid his head on the ground.

Culaina turned, and smiled. The whole clearing seemed to smile with her. The change was sudden, and dramatic.

'So here you are,' she said, 'and now you must tell me of your adventures. I know you will, because I remember you did. Follow me. There will be food.'

At the far side of the clearing was Culaina's home, or one of her homes. It was no more than a roof of woven dust on poles. There were no walls or doors, no ditch or stockade to protect it at night, and no place for a fire. Above it was a large hive of hymetors. Animals cropped and dozed peacefully around Culaina's camp.

When Glurk and the others approached the hymetors hummed furiously and rose from their hive in an angry swarm. The four ducked and tried to protect their faces with their arms, until Culaina whistled once.

The creatures swooped harmlessly overhead and returned, peacefully, to their home in the hairs. Glurk caught a glimpse of long sharp stings.

'She sent them back,' whispered Brocando urgently. 'She just whistled and they obeyed her!'

On the floor under the shelter was a pile of fruit and some bowls of green liquid.

'I had this before,' said Glurk. 'It's sap from the green hairs. Sets you up a treat.'

They sat down. Pismire shifted uneasily, and Culaina smiled at him.

'Say what you think,' she said. 'I remember that you did. But you must say it.'

'Wight mustn't tell people the future!' said Pismire. 'Everyone knows that! They *never* tell! It's too dangerous for people to know what will happen! This is all—'

'I remember I interrupted you here,' said the wight. 'Yes. I know the rules. And that's what they are, and *all* they are. They are only rules. I am not, Pismire, quite like other wights. Have you ever heard the word . . . thunorg? I know you have.'

'Oh, yes, the wights who can remember things that – oh. My word,' said Pismire, shocked, 'I thought that was just a story. I thought thunorgs were monsters.'

'It *is* just a story. But that doesn't mean it isn't true. The rules don't apply to me. *They're only rules*. Rules don't have to apply . . . not always. I don't much care for cities. But this crushing and destruction of the Carpet . . . this forging of bronze and trampling of dust . . .'

She shook her head. 'No. This shall not be. You will go to Ware tomorrow, before the mouls leave Jeopard. There will be a battle. You must win. I will not tell you how. But you must win. In the meantime, you may spend this night here. Do not be afraid. Nothing comes to my house that I do not expect.'

'No,' said Bane, 'I need to know. Why are you helping us? Wights remember everything that's ever happened, and what will happen. And they don't tell. What's different about you?'

Culaina put her head on one side.

'Did you hear me?' said Bane.

'Yes. I was remembering what I told you. Yes. Now I remember. There is so much, you see . . . so much . . .'

She stood up and walked a little way away from them. Then she turned. 'Pismire should know this,' she said. 'Sometimes . . . very rarely, as rare as my albino snarg here . . . sometimes a wight is born who is different, as different from wights as they are from you. You see, we remember . . . everything.'

'So do all wights,' said Bane.

'No,' said Culaina. 'They remember only all those things that happen. We remember things that *might* happen. I remember what will happen if you don't win. I know all possibilities. For every thing that happens, a million things don't happen. I live all of them. I remember you winning, and I remember you losing. I remember the mouls triumphant, I remember you triumphant. Both are real, for me. For me, both of these have happened. My brother and sister wights remember the thread of history. But I remember all the threads that never get woven. For me, all possibilities are real. I live in them all.'

'But why?' said Bane.

'Someone must. Otherwise, they never could have happened.'

She stepped into the shadows.

They heard her voice. It seemed to come from somewhere distant. 'Nothing *has* to happen. History isn't something you live. It is something you make. One decision. One person. At the right time. Nothing is too small to make a difference. Anything can be changed.'

The voice faded. After a while Bane got to his feet, feeling very clumsy, and peered into the shadows.

'She's gone.'

'I wonder if she can ever be entirely in one place,' said Pismire. 'What do we do now?'

'I'm going to sleep,' said Glurk, 'I don't know about you, but it's been a busy day.'

Several times Bane awoke, and thought he heard crashes

and cries in the wind, but when he listened hard they seemed to disappear.

Pismire dreamed. He saw hairs bend and bowing as if shaken by a high wind, and the gleam of ten thousand eyes, green, red and white, and the figure of Culaina, her hair caught and tugged by the air, treading through the noisy darkness, living everything that could be and might be and was.

Glurk dreamed of slim bodies pushing swiftly through the undergrowth. As they passed the Carpet seemed to come alive. It was like a splash in a cup; the ripples ran out and out, getting bigger as they ran. Deep in underground caves sleeping creatures awoke, and howled. He saw the Thimbrule that lay far beyond Varnisholme, a great silver dome. He saw the glow as the wights mined their varnish at Varnisholme, the flames spouting from their forge.

In his dream he moved through the night hairs like a spirit, until he came to the Endless Flatness. The Carpet ended suddenly, and from its shores the Flatness ran on for ever. He looked for hairs and there were none, just flatness without end, and balls of dust that were bowled over and over in the forlorn wind. And Culaina stood by the last hair, her robe flapping in the gusts.

Glurk sat up suddenly.

It was morning. Yellow light dappled the clearing, making the hairs shine like bronze. Brocando was still asleep. The others were talking quietly.

One look was enough.

'Not exactly dreams,' said Pismire. 'What we dreamed weren't exactly dreams. She lives all her lives at once, we picked up echoes—'

'I saw Culaina walking through the Carpet,' began Glurk. 'And I think I saw Snibril, too.'

'And I saw the Hearthlands and the fire in the sky,' added Pismire.

'There were all sorts of creatures,' said Glurk.

111

Brocando turned over and opened his eyes. He listened to the others for a moment, then nodded. 'I was back in the High Gate Land. There was a domed cave, and under the dome a throne of bronze with a Vortgorn on it. He had a yellow beard and a crown. Two mouls were standing in front of him. I'll swear one of them was Gormaleesh. They were laughing. Then one snatched the crown, but the Vortgorn just sat with his chin on his hand and said nothing.'

'That'd be Stagbat, their king,' said Glurk. 'I heard the Vortgorn guards talking. The mouls turned up one day after Fray had struck nearby and they said Fray was a Dumii weapon. They said they'd be *allies*. Now they run the place, of course.'

'You can't control Fray,' said Pismire. 'I keep on telling you, it's a natural phenomenon.'

'They always find our weak points,' said Glurk. He looked across at Bane, who had been silent.

'And what did *you* dream?' he asked.

'I dreamed . . . I dreamed . . .' Bane began, and then seemed to wake up, 'I dreamed of nothing. I slept well.'

There was no sign of Culaina. The pones had stayed.

'They think life is going to be interesting,' said Glurk. 'They used to like working for the Vortgorns. People used to come and read them stories and things. Must be hard, having a brain and no hands to do things with it.'

'We'd better go to Ware,' said Bane. 'I don't think we've got any choice.'

'We've got lots of choice,' said Pismire. 'It's just that we've got to choose to go to Ware.'

Glurk saddled up Acretongue. 'Interesting times ahead,' he said gloomily.

Bane took a last look around the sugar clearing.

'She's here . . . somewhere,' he said.

'Everywhere,' said Pismire. 'Everywhere there's a choice to be made.'

There was a faraway look in Bane's eyes. 'What must it be like,' he said, 'to know everything that could happen?'

'Terrible,' said Pismire. 'Now, come along. Bane? I said come on . . .'

Chapter 14

Snibril had led the search, after the storm. They'd sifted through the rubble of the place. They'd gone down into Underlay, roped together, and shouted out the names of those who were lost. They'd found nothing.

But as Pismire would have pointed out, finding nothing was better than finding . . . something.

Then they'd discovered the tracks in the distant clearing. Lots of creatures had come up. It seemed to Snibril that there had been someone else following them, someone who had lain low for a while in the bushes . . . but everything was covered with dust shaken down by the storm, and it was hard to be sure. The tracks, such as they were, led south.

The Munrungs had helped Brocando's people rebuild walls and things, even though the rock itself was now visibly leaning over. And, as someone said, if Fray came again at least they now knew how to get into Underlay. Nothing would get them there.

Snibril thought about this as he rode Roland through the hairs, looking for any more tracks.

We can always go into Underlay, he thought. We can stop being people. We can just grub around in the dark.

The Deftmenes think that no enemy is too big to fight, but we never even *see* Fray.

The Dumii don't think like that. They think that if an enemy is too big, you should find a smaller enemy.

Maybe Pismire is right. We can't stop Fray. But at least we can stop being frightened of Fray.

'I'm going to Ware,' he told the tribe that evening. They looked at him in horror. Technically, Glurk was still chief . . . if he was alive. If he wasn't, then Snibril was chief. Glurk's children were all too young. No-one wanted to lose another chief.

'You can't leave us,' said Dodor Plint, who was the tribe's shoemaker. 'You're the leader.'

'Ware's important,' said Snibril. 'We'd just be simple hunters if it wasn't for the Empire.'

The Munrungs looked at one another.

'We *are* simple hunters,' said Plint.

'Yes, but at least we *know* we are,' said Snibril. 'Anyway, we've got more complicated.'

'That's true,' said Crooly Wulf, who was nearly as old as Pismire. 'People don't hit one another over the head with clubs as much as they did when I was a boy. There's more arguing.'

'That doesn't mean we're better people!' said Plint.

Crooly Wulf rubbed his head. 'I dunno,' he said. 'People are taller now. They don't groan so much, either.'

'Huh! But the Deftmenes don't have anything to do with the Dumii,' said Plint. 'And they manage.'

'They fight them,' said Snibril, simply. 'It's amazing how things rub off, even when you fight people. Ideas like . . . like not just killing people all the time, that sort of thing.'

A Deftmene put up his hand.

'That's true,' he said. 'The kings always used to throw people off the rock in the old days.'

'He still does,' said another Deftmene.

'Yes, but he doesn't laugh about it so much. And he says he's doing it for their own good.'

'See?' said Snibril desperately. 'The Dumii have an effect. Even if you're their enemy. I'm going south.

Perhaps I can find the others. Perhaps the Empire can help us.'

'Yes, but you're our leader—' Plint began again.

'Then I'm going to lead!' snapped Snibril. 'Who else is coming?'

Some of the younger Munrungs raised their hands.

A Deftmene stood up. 'Will there be fighting against impossible odds?' he said.

'Probably,' said Snibril.

'Right! Count us in!' A lot of Deftmenes nodded. Another one said: 'And will we get a chance to fight to the death?'

'You might get a chance to fight to the *enemy's* death,' said Snibril.

'Is that as good?'

'Better.'

'Right, then. We're with you!'

In the end three hundred and fifty Deftmenes and fifty Munrungs volunteered to go. On the Rock their families would be as safe as anywhere in the Carpet, they agreed, but someone had to stay. Anything could happen.

Four hundred, thought Snibril. Who knows how many we're going to face?

On the other hand, since we don't know how many we're going to face, four hundred might be just enough.

Always choose a bigger enemy. It makes him easier to hit.

We must go to Ware. It's where we all began, in a way. It's where people first realized that there may be a better way of doing things than hitting one another on the head.

Chapter 15

It was two days later.

In a grove of red hairs on the borders of the blue land seven wights were fighting mouls. It was unheard of for wights to be attacked.

They never carried weapons, apart from the ones they were making for sale.

This moul pack was large, and led by a chieftain more cunning and wily than most. What he wanted was more weapons. Wights looked easy prey.

He was beginning to regret this decision.

The wights didn't carry weapons, but they did carry tools. And a hammer *is* a weapon, if you hit a head instead of a nail. They were standing around their big varnish-boiler and fighting back – *hammering* back, and using varnish ladles as clubs, and bits of burning hair as crude spears.

But they were outnumbered. And they were all going to die. They *knew* it.

There was someone watching who knew it too.

Culaina the thunorg watched from deep in the hairs. It would be impossible to describe how a thunorg sees things. It would be like trying to explain the stars to a fish. How can it be said that she watched the fight a million times, all at the same instant, and every time the wights lost? It's the wrong description. But it will have to do.

But among all the outcomes there was just one, as alone as a pearl on a seashore of black sand, that was different.

She turned without moving, and concentrated on it—

The hairs erupted people. The mouls turned to fight, but suddenly they were between two enemies.

The Deftmenes and the Munrungs had found an unbeatable fighting method. The tall Munrungs stood behind the small Deftmenes and fought over the top of them; no enemy had much of a chance on two levels at once.

It was a short fight, and a terribly effective one.

After a few minutes, the remaining mouls ran for it. Some of the new attackers broke away to follow them.

And then it was over – in this one pearl-on-a-seashore time, when someone whose whole life was a choice had been close enough to choose.

Athan the kilnmaster, leader of this band, looked up with horror as a white horse trotted through the lines of his rescuers. There was a small figure riding it.

'How can this be! We were supposed to die!' he said. 'All of us!'

'Did you want to?' said Snibril, dismounting.

'Want? *Want?* That doesn't come into it,' said Athan, throwing down his hammer. From out in the hairs came the screech of a moul.

'You changed things,' said Athan. 'And now terrible things will happen—'

'They don't have to,' said Snibril, calmly. 'Nothing *has* to happen. You can *let* things happen. But that's not the same. We're going to Ware. There's Munrungs and Deftmenes and a few other refugees we picked up along the way. Why not come?'

Athan looked shocked and angry. 'Us? *Wights?* Fighting?'

'You were fighting just now.'

'Yes, but we knew we would lose,' said Athan.

'How about fighting and hoping you'll win?' said Snibril. He turned as a Munrung approached, carrying a wight.

'Our Geridan is dead, and one of the Deftmenes,' said the Munrung. 'And one of the wights. But this one's still alive . . . just.'

'That is Derna,' said Athan. 'My . . . daughter. She should be dead. In a way . . . she *must be* dead . . .'

'We have some medicines,' said Snibril quietly. 'Or we could bury her now, if that's what you want . . .'

He looked expectantly at the kilnmaster, who had gone white.

'No,' he said, almost in a whisper.

'Good. Because we wouldn't have done it anyway,' said Snibril briskly. 'And then you'll come with us.'

'But I don't . . . know . . . what will happen next,' said the wight. 'I can't remember!'

'You joined us and went to Ware,' said Snibril.

'I *can't remember what's going to happen*!'

'You joined us,' Snibril repeated.

Relief flooded across Athan's face. Suddenly he looked frantically happy, like a child who has been given a new toy. 'Did I?' he said.

'Why not?' said Snibril. 'It must be better than being dead.'

'But this . . . this is thunorg thinking,' said Athan. 'The future is The Future, not . . . not . . .' he hesitated, baffled, '. . . not . . . perhaps . . . really? The future can be all different things—?'

'Pick your own,' said Snibril.

'But destiny—'

'That's something you make up as you go along,' said Snibril. 'I've been finding that out.'

He looked up at a faint sound, faint enough not to be heard except by someone who was a hunter and whose life depended on noticing tiny noises. For a moment he thought he saw a pale figure in the shadows, smiling at him. Then it vanished.

Geridan was buried among the hairs with the Deftmene noble Parleon, son of Leondo, killed by a snarg, and the wight who had died.

The remaining wights huddled amongst themselves, and Snibril could hear them arguing. But he knew he'd won. They hadn't got a future any more. They had to have the one he'd given Athan. They weren't used to making them for themselves.

They cast the last of the hot varnish into swords and spearheads, and piled them up so that the ragged army could help themselves. and when the army left they went too, leaving the cart alone and cold.

A million times the wights lost, and were killed. But that was somewhere else, in a world that might have been. And now they were alive. And that's known as History, which is only written by the living.

Chapter 16

They went by narrow tracks that wound in and out of overgrown thickets. In some places enormous hairs had fallen over the path. Dust and fluff grew thickly, choking the spaces between hairs so that they could only move by hacking their way through undergrowth that clawed and pricked them.

Once, in a patch of thick orange hairs, something hurtled out of the tangled bushes and buried itself in a hair bole by Snibril's head. It was a spear.

Up in the hairs a shadow scampered, swinging to safety on a creeper while Deftmene arrows whined around it like hymetors. They never found out what it was, although it might have had something to do with the fact that, a little later, they found a city.

It was not on any maps of the Carpet. For some time they had been walking through its overgrown streets, not realizing they were streets, until they found the statues. Little blue dust flowers grew on them, and fluff had planted itself around them, but they still stood in the centre of their lost city. They had been four kings; wooden crowns were on their wooden heads and they each pointed with one arm to a different point of the compass. Ferns grew around their feet, and small creatures had made their homes in crooks of arms and folds of carven clothing.

Around them, when you knew what you were looking

for in the way the hairs grew and dust mounds were banked, was the city. Age hung upon it like smoke. Thick hairs grew in the ruins of buildings, dust had filled the streets. Creepers and tendrils had done their work, breaking down walls and venturing into hidden walls. Insects chirruped in broken archways. Hair pollen made the air sparkle.

'Do you know this place?' said Snibril.

No-one did. Even Athan had never heard of it.

'Places can get lost,' he said. 'People leave. Hairs grow up. Roads are overgrown.'

'By the look of those statues, they thought the place would last for ever,' said Snibril.

'It didn't,' said Athan, flatly.

And now they've gone, thought Snibril. Or there's just a few left, hunting around in the remains of their city. No-one knows who they were, or what they did. No-one even remembers their name. That mustn't happen to us.

The wights weren't talkative now. It must be like being blind, Snibril thought. *We're* used to not knowing what's going to happen . . .

A couple of hours later they reached a Dumii road. It was white, made of split hairs laid edge to edge. Every few hundred yards there was a hair carved with a finger. All the fingers pointed to Ware.

They rode along it a little way. Here and there the road had been broken when the Carpet had moved, and they had to take to the hairs to get around the break.

That's where they found the legion, or what was left of it. Dumii soldiers were sitting or lying amongst the hairs by the side of the road. Some of them were asleep. Others were wounded.

He'd seen plenty of soldiers in Tregon Marus, but they had simply been on guard. These looked *battered*, their uniforms ragged and often blood-stained.

They hardly bothered to look up as Snibril rode by.

But the ones who did caught sight of the Deftmenes, and started nudging their colleagues. One or two even reached for their swords.

There was muttering from the Deftmenes, too. They moved closer together, and eyed the Dumii suspiciously.

Snibril turned in his saddle.

'Don't make any trouble,' he snapped.

'Why not?' said a sullen voice from among the Deftmene ranks. 'They're Dumii!'

'You'd prefer them to be mouls, would you?'

He walked Roland over to a group of soldiers sitting on a fallen hair.

'Where is your leader?' he said.

The Dumii looked him up and down.

'Haven't got one,' he said. 'General got killed.'

There was a pause.

'I expect you're wondering who we are,' said Snibril.

'Too tired to wonder,' said the soldier, leaning back against a hair.

'Stand up straight!'

For a moment Snibril wondered who had said that. Then he realized that it had been him.

To his amazement, the soldier pulled himself upright.

'Now take me to the highest-ranking officer!' said Snibril. I musn't say 'please', he thought. I mustn't give him a chance to think. He's used to orders. It's easier for him to obey orders than think.

'Er . . . that'd be Sergeant Careus. If he's still alive.'

'Take me to him *now*!'

The soldier looked past Snibril at the ragged army. His forehead wrinkled.

'I shall talk to the sergeant!' said Snibril. The soldier snapped back to attention.

'Yessir. This way,' he said.

Snibril was led past groups of sullen soldiers to a heavy-set man who was sitting on the ground. One arm

123

was in a sling, and his face was pale. He didn't seem to be bothered about who Snibril actually was. He was feeling low enough to accept anyone who seemed to know what they were doing.

'Sergeant Careus, Fifteenth Legion,' he said, 'Or what's left of it. We were called back to Ware urgently from Ultima Marus, but when we were on the road—'

'—there was a storm—' said Snibril automatically.

'And then afterwards—'

'—you were attacked by mouls mounted on snargs,' said Snibril.

'Yes. Time and again. How did you know this?'

'I'm good at guessing,' said Snibril. 'How many of you are there?'

'About three hundred able-bodied, and a lot of wounded.'

'I know a safe city where your wounded can be taken. It's only two days' easy march, if we spare some soldiers to escort them.'

'We'll need too many,' said the sergeant. 'There'll be mouls everywhere.'

'Not where *we've* been,' said Snibril quietly. 'Not any more. And the rest of us will go with you to Ware.'

The sergeant looked down at the dust, thinking. 'I won't say we don't need everyone we can get,' he said. 'Where's this paradise, then?'

'Jeopard,' said Snibril.

'You must be mad!'

At that moment there was a roar from the road. Both of them hurried back, to where there was now a huge pushing crowd of Dumii and Deftmenes, with the Munrungs trying to keep them apart. Snibril pushed his way through and found a Deftmene and a soldier rolling over and over on the road, punching at one another.

Snibril watched them for a moment, and then flung his spear on the ground.

'Stop that!' he shouted. 'You're soldiers! You're not supposed to fight!'

Even the two combatants stopped to work that one out.

'I don't understand you!' Snibril shouted. His voice echoed off the hairs. 'There's enemies all around us, and you just attack each other! Why?'

'They're closer,' said a voice from the Dumii ranks.

'He called me dirty!' said the Deftmene who had been fighting.

'Well, you are,' said Snibril. 'So's he. We all are. Now get up—'

He stopped. All the Dumii were looking past him, to Athan and the wights, and Snibril heard the whispering start.

'They've got wights with them . . . fighting!'

He looked at Athan, who looked miserable. Snibril sidled over to him.

'Don't let them know you can't remember this future,' he said.

'They know the future! And they're on his side!'

'Why should we fight for them if they treat us like that?' said a Deftmene. Snibril spun around and picked up the astonished warrior by his collar.

'You're not fighting for them! You're fighting for yourselves!'

The Deftmene was shaken, but not afraid. 'We've always fought for ourselves,' he said, 'And we were never Counted!'

'No, but the Empire was all around you, wasn't it, keeping you safe! The Dumii kept the peace over half the Carpet! All around you! Kept you safe!'

'They never did!'

'Think about it! There's Dumii towns all around you!

125

When they defended themselves, they were defending you! They fought for real so that you could fight them for fun!'

Snibril was shaking with anger.

There was silence.

He put the Deftmene down.

'I'm going to Ware,' he said. 'Anyone else wants to come, it's up to them . . .'

No-one left, except for a small group who were going to accompany the wounded back to Jeopard. Two of the wights went with them. The Dumii felt a lot better with wights around. They seemed to think that wights only went where it was safe. That's what *they'd* do . . .

The rest of them marched on down the road. Snibril found that he was in command; the Munrungs wanted to follow him, the Deftmenes were beginning to think that anyone who could lose their temper that badly was probably a king, and the Dumii – well, the Dumii soldiers followed Sergeant Careus, and Sergeant Careus was riding alongside Snibril. Most armies are in fact run by their sergeants – the officers are there just to give things a bit of tone and prevent warfare becoming a mere lower-class brawl.

The sergeant half turned in his saddle and looked back at the Deftmenes.

'Nice to have cavalry on our side again,' he said. 'Even if they're still shorter than infantry. I've fought against them a couple of times. Tough little ba . . . people. That was under Baneus. He respected 'em. He left 'em alone. They didn't like that back in Ware, but he always said it's worth keeping a few enemies around. You know. To practise on. I think he quite liked 'em. Odd little ba . . . chaps.'

'Baneus,' said Snibril, cautiously. 'Yes. Er. Whatever happened to him? Did he do something terrible?'

'You know him?'

'I've . . . heard of him,' said Snibril carefully.

'He killed someone. An assassin. The way I heard it, someone was trying to kill the young Emperor during his coronation. Hiding behind a pillar with a bow. Baneus spotted him and threw his sword at him. Got him just in time. Killed him grit dead. Arrow missed Targon by inches. Funny thing is, Baneus hated Targon. He was always in trouble. He said Emperors shouldn't be hereditary, but elected just like they used to be. A stickler for honesty, was the General. Oh, there were always rows. But after that, he had to be banished, of course.'

'Why of course?' said Snibril.

'No-one is allowed to draw a sword within fifty paces of the Emperor,' said the Sergeant.

'But he saved his life!'

'Yes, but you've got to have rules, otherwise where would we be?' said Sergeant Careus.

'But—'

'Afterwards the Emperor had the law changed and they sent someone after the General.'

'Did he ever find him?'

'I think so. He was sent back tied to his horse with an apple in his mouth. I think the General was a bit upset.'

The Deftmenes are mad and the Dumii are sane, thought Snibril, and that's just the same as being mad except that it's quieter. If only you could mix them together, you'd end up with normal people. Just like me.

'We could do with him now, and that's a fact,' said the sergeant.

'Yes,' said Snibril. 'Um. What do I do now? We'll have to camp tonight. I mean, I don't know what sort of orders you're supposed to give.'

The sergeant looked at him kindly.

'You say "Make camp here",' he said.

Chapter 17

A scattering of campfires speckled the darkness. It was the second night of the journey of all four races. No-one had killed anyone yet.

Snibril and the sergeant had made sure that there was at least one Munrung at each campfire, as referees.

'I wish we could get some more wights fighting,' said Careus. 'I watched one of them using a bow just now, when the lads were practising. I mean, when have they ever used a bow before? He just looked at it for a while, then put an arrow in the centre of the target. Just like that.'

'Just as well they don't fight, then,' said Snibril. 'Maybe it's best to leave it to people who aren't so good at it. What's the plan?'

'Plan?' said Careus. 'I *don't* know. I just fight. Fought all my life. Always been a soldier. All I know is what the messenger said . . . all the legions are going back to Ware.'

'All fifteen?' said Snibril. He rubbed his head It was feeling . . . sort of squashed . . .

The sergeant looked surprised. 'Fifteen? We haven't got fifteen. Oh, yes. We're *called* the Fifteenth. But a lot got disbanded. No need for 'em, see? Hardly anyone left to fight. It's like that, empiring. One day you're fighting everyone, next day everyone's settled down and being lawful and you don't hardly need soldiers.'

'So how many are there?' said Snibril.

'Three.'

'Three legions? How many people is that?'

'About three thousand men.'

'Is that all?'

Careus shrugged. 'Less than that now, I reckon. All scattered around, too.'

'But that's not enough to—' Snibril stopped, and then raised his hands slowly to his head. 'Tell everyone to lie down,' he muttered. 'Put out their fires and lie down!'

One or two horses started to whinny in the picket lines.

'Why?' said the sergeant. 'What's the—'

'And they must be ready to fight!' said Snibril. His head felt as though someone was treading on it. He could hardly think. Somewhere in the hairs, an animal screeched.

Careus was looking at him as if he was ill. 'What's the—' he began.

'*Please!* Can't explain! Do it now!'

Careus ran off. He could hear him shouting orders to the corporals. The Deftmenes and Munrungs didn't need telling twice.

A moment later, Fray struck.

It was away to the south . . . not far. The pressure built up so that even the Dumii could feel it. The hairs bowed, and then whipped furiously as a wind blew clouds of dust through the Carpet. The soldiers who hadn't been quick enough to follow orders were picked up and bowled over and over in the dust.

And then there was the thump.

Afterwards, there was that long, crowded pause in which everyone decides that although they are very shaken, and possibly upside down, they are, to their surprise, still alive.

Careus crawled around until he found his helmet

under a bush and then, still not standing up, shuffled over to Snibril.

'You felt it coming,' he said. 'Even before the animals!'

'The mouls can, too,' said Snibril. 'And they're better at it than me! They don't summon Fray! They can sense when it's going to happen! And then they attack afterwards, when everyone's shaken—'

He and Careus looked around at the hairs.

'To arms, everyone!' the sergeant yelled.

A Deftmene raised his hand. 'What does that mean?' he said. 'We've *all* got two arms.'

'Means you've got to fight!'

'Oh, *right*.'

It was only seconds later that the mouls attacked. But seconds were enough. A hundred of them galloped into what should have been a camp of bewildered, wounded and unprepared victims. They found instead bewildered, wounded and extremely well-prepared and moreover enraged fighters.

They were surprised. But their surprise didn't last long. It was, very accurately, the surprise of their life

The moul attack changed things. Deftmenes and Dumii had always fought, but never on the same side. It's hard to feel so bad about someone when last night he was stopping other people hitting you with axes and things.

The little army swung down the road to Ware, singing. Admittedly there were three different marching songs, all to different tunes, but the general effect was quite harmonious if you didn't mind not being able to make out any of the words.

'The lads sing one about me sometimes,' said the sergeant. 'It's got seven verses. Some of them are very rude, and one of them is actually impossible. I have to

130

pretend not to hear it. Have you noticed the wights ran away in the night?'

'Not ran away,' said Snibril. 'I don't think they've run away. That doesn't sound like them. I think . . . they've decided to do something else.'

'They went into a huddle after the fight,' said the sergeant.

'Perhaps they've got a plan—' Snibril began.

He stopped.

They had been passing through the area that had been right under Fray. Hairs were bent and twisted. And over the road was an arch. Had *been* an arch.

There were some dead soldiers nearby, and one dead moul.

The legion spread out in silence, watching the hairs. A squad was sent off to bury the dead.

'That could have been us, without you,' said Careus. 'How much warning do you get?'

'A minute or two, that's all,' said Snibril. 'Perhaps a bit longer if it's quiet.'

'What does it feel like?'

'Like someone's treading on my head! What is this place?'

'One of the gates to the Ware lands. The city's further on.'

'I've always wondered what it looked like,' said Snibril.

'Me too,' said the sergeant.

'You mean you've never seen it?' said Snibril.

'No. Born in a garrison town, see. Done all my soldiering around and about. Never been to Ware. Heard it's very impressive, though. A nice place to visit,' said Careus. 'We should be there in a few hours.'

'Ware!' said Snibril.

Chapter 18

Ware had been built between and round five giant hairs. There were really three cities, ringed one inside the other. Inside the thick outer walls was Imperial Ware, a city of wide avenues paved with wood and salt, lined with statues, a city of impressive vistas and magnificent buildings, and at every turn monuments to old battles and glorious victories and even one or two defeats of the more glorious sort.

Few people actually lived in Imperial Ware, except a few caretakers and gardeners and dozens of sculptors. It was a city for looking at, not living in.

Outside it, separated by a wall of sharpened hair stakes, was Merchants' Ware, the city most people thought of as the real city. Normally its narrow streets were crowded with stalls, and people from all over the Carpet. They'd all be trying to cheat one another in that open-and-above-board way known as 'doing business'. All sorts of languages could be heard, often very loudly. Ware was where people came to trade.

The Dumii had built their Empire with swords, but they kept it with money. They'd invented money. Before money, people had bought things with cows and pigs, which were not very efficient for the purpose because you had to feed them and keep them safe all the time and sometimes they died. And suddenly the Dumii turned up with this money stuff, which was small and easy to keep and you could hide it in a sock under the mattress, which hardly ever worked with cows and pigs. And it could *be* cows or pigs. Also, it had little pictures of Emperors and things on it, which were interesting to look at. At least, more interesting than cows and pigs.

And, Pismire had once said, *that* was how the Dumii kept their Empire. Because once you started using Dumii money, which was so easy and convenient and didn't moo all night, you started saving up for things, and selling things in the nearest market town, and settling down, and not hitting neighbouring tribes as often as you used to. And you could buy things in the markets that you'd never seen before – coloured cloth, and different kinds of fruit, and books. Pretty soon, you were doing things the Dumii way, *because it made life better*. Oh, you went on about how much better life was in the old days, before there was all this money and peacefulness around, and how much more enjoyable things were when people used to get heavily-armed in the evenings and go out and make their own entertainment – but no-one was anxious actually to go back there.

'Economic imperialism!' Pismire had once said, picking up a handful of coins. 'A marvellous idea. So neat and simple. Once you set it going, it works all by itself. You see, it's the *Emperor* who guarantees that the money will buy you things. Every time someone hands over or accepts one of these coins, it's a little soldier defending the Empire. Amazing!'

No-one understood a word of what he meant, but they could see he thought it was important.

And then, off to one side of the bustling city, was a tiny walled enclosure, about the size of a village.

This was Ware. The first Ware. The little village where the Dumii had begun. No-one really knew how, or why Destiny had picked this one little tribe and then wound them up like a big rubber band and sent them out to conquer the world. Hardly anyone went into old Ware these days. Probably it'd soon be pulled down, to make room for some more statues.

Snibril didn't see Old Ware until much later. He saw the walls of the city, stretching away on either side. He could see the glint of armour on the walls, too, as the sentries marched sedately along. Everything looked peaceful, as if something like Fray had never existed.

Careus took off his helmet and surreptitiously gave it a bit of a polish. 'There could be trouble if we try to take the Deftmenes in,' he whispered to Snibril.

'Not could,' Snibril agreed. 'Would.'

'So we'll camp outside for now. You better come on in with me.'

Snibril scanned the walls. 'It's all so quiet and peaceful,' he said. 'I thought there'd be a war! Why were you called back?'

'That's what I'm here to find out,' said Careus. He spat on his hand and tried to flatten his hair a bit. 'Something's not right,' he said. 'You know how you can sense when there's going to be an attack by Fray?'

'Yes.'

'I'm the same way about trouble. Which is what there's going to be. I can feel it. Come on.'

Snibril rode after the sergeant through the streets. It looked normal. At least, it looked as he thought it'd probably look if things were normal. It was like Tregon Marus, only bigger. Much bigger. He tried to keep up, among the crowds that filled the streets, and tried to look as if it was all familiar.

Whenever he'd thought of Ware, when he was younger, he'd imagined a kind of glow around it. It was the way people spoke about it. He imagined Ware as all kinds of strange places, but he'd never imagined this – that it was simply a much bigger version of an ordinary town, with more people and statues.

Careus led him to a barracks just outside the Imperial city, and eventually they reached a table, out in the open air, at which a skinny little Dumii was sitting behind a pile of papers. Messengers kept picking up some from the table, but others kept on bringing new ones. He looked harassed.

'Yes?' he demanded.

'I am—' the sergeant began.

'I don't know, people barge in here, I expect you haven't even got any papers, have you? No? Of course you haven't.' The little man shuffled his own papers irritably. 'They expect me to keep track, how can I keep track, is this how you're supposed to run an army? Well, come on, name and rank, name and rank . . .'

The sergeant raised his hand. For a moment Snibril thought he was going to hit the skinny man, but instead it turned into a salute.

'Sergeant Careus, Fifteenth Legion,' he said. 'We're outside the city, those of us who are left. Do you understand? I'm seeking permission to come into the barracks. We've fought—'

'Fifteenth Legion, Fifteenth Legion,' said the skinny man, shuffling through the papers.

'We were summoned back,' said Careus. 'There was a messenger. Return at once to Ware. We had to fight most of—'

'There have been a lot of changes,' said the paper shuffler.

There was a tone in his voice that affected Snibril almost as much as the approach of Fray.

'What sort of changes?' he said quickly. The man looked at him.

'Who's this?' he said suspiciously. 'Looks a bit . . . native to me.'

135

'Look,' said Careus patiently, 'We've come all the way back because—'

'Oh, this Fray business,' said the skinny man. 'All sorted out. There's been a treaty.'

'A treaty? With *Fray*?' said Snibril.

'A peace treaty with the mouls, of course. Don't you know *anything*?'

Snibril opened his mouth. Careus gripped his arm. 'Oh,' he said, loudly and distinctly. 'Well. Isn't that nice. We won't disturb you further. Come, Snibril.'

'But—!'

'I'm sure this gentleman has got some very important things to do with his paper,' said the sergeant.

'Why did you do that?' said Snibril, as the sergeant hurried him out.

'Because if we want to find out things, we won't find 'em out by making that clerk eat all his little bits of paper,' said Careus. 'We'll spy around for a while, get the lie of the land, find out what's going on – and maybe later on we can come *back* and make him eat all his bits of paper.'

'I haven't even seen many other soldiers!' said Snibril.

'Just a few guards,' agreed Careus, as they hurried out into the street.

'The other legions can't have got here yet,' said Snibril.

'Do you think they will?' said Careus.

'What do you mean?'

'We met you and the little people. If we hadn't, I don't think we would have made it,' said Careus gloomily.

'You mean . . . we're all there is?'

'Could be.'

And we're less than a thousand of us, Snibril thought. How can you have a peace treaty with mouls? They just destroy things. How could they be here, making treaties?

* * *

136

The army camped out among the hairs. As one of the Deftmenes said, it was hard to feel at ease surrounded by enemies, especially when they were on your own side. But at least he grinned when he said it.

It was while groups of them picked up firewood among the hairs that they found the pones.

There were a dozen of them. Pones could hide quite easily in the Carpet. They were so big. People think that it's easiest to hide things that are small, but it's almost as easy to hide things that are too big to see. The pones just looked like mounds, except that they were chewing the cud and burping occasionally. They all turned their heads to look at their discoverers, burped, and then looked away.

They looked as if they'd been told to wait for someone.

The sign outside the shop said Apothecary, which meant that the shop was owned by a sort of early chemist, who would give you herbs and things until you got better or at least stopped getting any worse.

The apothecary's name was Owlglass. He hummed to himself as he worked in his back room. He'd found a new type of blue fluff, which he was grinding down. It was probably good for curing something. He'd have to try it out on people until he found out what.

A hand touched him on the shoulder.

'Hmm?' he said.

He turned around. He peered over the top of his spectacles, which were made out of two circles of carefully-shaped varnish.

'*Pismire?*' he said.

'Keep your voice down! We came in the back way,' said Pismire.

'My word, I expect you did,' said Owlglass. 'Don't worry, there's no-one in the shop.' He looked past the old man, to Glurk and Bane and Brocando. 'My word,' he said again. 'After all this time, eh? Well . . . welcome. My house is your house,' his brow suddenly furrowed and he looked worried, 'although only in a metaphorical sense, you understand, because I would not, much as I always admired your straightforward approach, and indeed your forthright stance, actually *give* you my house, it being the only house I have, and therefore the term is being extended in an, as it were, gratuitous fashion—'

Owlglass was clearly having some trouble getting to the end of the sentence. Glurk tapped Pismire on the shoulder.

'He's a philosopher too, is he?' he said.

'You can tell, can't you,' said Pismire. 'Um, Owlglass . . . thanks very much.'

The apothecary gave up the struggle, and smiled.

'We need some food,' said Pismire. 'And most of all—'

'—we want information,' said Bane. 'What's happening here?'

'Which would you like first?' said Owlglass.

'Food,' said Glurk. The others glared at him. 'Well, I thought he was looking at me when he asked,' he said.

'Make yourself at home,' said Owlglass, 'Although of course when I say *home* I don't precisely mean—'

'Yes, yes, thank you very much,' said Pismire. Owlglass bustled over to a cupboard. Glurk stared at the jars and pots that littered the back room. In some of the jars, things stared back.

'Owlglass and I went to school together,' said Pismire. 'And then Owlglass decided he was going to study the Carpet. What it's made of. The properties of different kinds of hair. Rare and strange animals. That sort of thing.'

'And Pismire decided he was going to study people,'

said Owlglass, producing a loaf and some butter. 'And got sentenced to death for calling the last Emperor a . . . a . . . what was it now?'

'Well, he deserved it,' said Pismire. 'He wouldn't give me any money to preserve the Library. All the books were crumbling. I was supposed to look after the Library, after all. It's *knowledge*. He said we didn't need a lot of old books, we knew all we needed to know. I was just trying to make the point that a civilisation needs books if there's going to be a reasoned and well-informed exchange of views.'

'I was trying to remember what you called him.'

'An ignorant sybarite who didn't have the sense of a meat pie,' said Pismire.

'Sounds pretty nasty, sentencing someone to death just for that,' said Glurk, putting the loaf on his plate. He kept turning around to look at the jar behind him. It had something hairy in it.

'Actually, he got sentenced to death for apologizing,' said Owlglass.

'How can you be sentenced to death for apologizing?'

'He said he was sorry, but on reflection he realized that the Emperor *had* got the sense of a meat pie,' said Owlglass. 'He was running at the time, too.'

'I think on my feet,' said Pismire, proudly.

'You insulted the Emperor?' said Brocando. 'Why didn't you say? I didn't know you were *famous*.'

'And accurate,' said Bane. 'Targon's father was a disgrace to the Empire.'

'Where have you been hiding all these years?' said Owlglass, pulling up a chair, 'Of course, when I say *hiding* I don't mean—'

'Oh, a little place no-one's ever heard of,' said Pismire.

'Do you mind if I turn that jar around?' said Glurk. 'I don't like things watching me when I eat.'

'What's happening here in Ware?' said Bane shortly. 'There's hardly a guard on the gates. That is disgusting. Don't people know what's happening? The Empire's being attacked. My empire!'

'If no-one wants that piece of cheese, pass it along,' said Glurk.

'We've heard,' said Owlglass. 'But the Emperor says that Ware is perfectly safe. These new advisers say so, apparently.'

'Advisers?' said Pismire. The word was like a lump of grit.

'There aren't any pickles around, are there?' said Glurk.

'Advisers,' said Bane. 'And has anyone . . . seen these advisers?'

'Don't think so,' said Owlglass. 'I heard that General Vagerus was demoted for calling the legions back. The Emperor said he was spreading unnecessary alarm. And the guards around the palace aren't letting anyone in.'

'Is there any more of this cucumber?'

'It's how *they* work,' said Bane. 'You *know* it. From inside. Like Jeopard. And the High Gate Land.'

'What? Cucumbers?' said Glurk.

'Yes, but not in Ware,' said Pismire. 'Not *here*. I can't believe that. Not at the centre. Surely not?'

'Who would think of looking at the centre?' said Bane.

'If it comes to that, I wouldn't have expected them in Jeopard,' said Brocando.

'Is this still about cucumbers?'

'Yes, but not . . . Ware,' said Pismire.

'You don't think so? I would have said the same about Jeopard,' said Brocando.

'Hardly anyone is allowed in the place these days,' said Owlglass.

'It's not cucumbers you're talking about, is it,' said Glurk.

'What can we do?' said Pismire.

'Slice 'em!' said Glurk, waving a cucumber.

Bane put his hand on his sword. 'Yes,' he said. 'I knew this would happen. Ware was a great city, once. We fought for things. And when we got them . . . we just sat back. No more effort. No more pride. No more honesty. Just fat young Emperors and stupid courtiers. Well, I'm not having that. Not in Ware. Let's go.' He stood up.

'Oh, no,' said Pismire. 'What are you going to do? Barge into the palace waving your sword and kill any mouls you see?'

Brocando stood up too. 'Good thinking,' he said. 'Good plan. Glad we've got that sorted out. Come on—'

'That's ridiculous!' said Pismire. 'That's not a plan! Tell them, Glurk. You're a level-headed man.'

'Yes, it *is* ridiculous,' said Glurk.

'Right,' said Pismire.

'We'll finish our tea,' said Glurk, 'and *then* attack the palace. It's no good attacking on an empty stomach.'

'Mad!' said Pismire.

'Listen,' said Bane, standing up, 'You know what *she* said. Nothing is too small to make a difference. One person at the right time.'

'There's three of us,' said Brocando.

'Even better!'

'Oh, *blast*! I suppose I'd better come,' sighed Pismire, 'if only to see you don't do anything *too* stupid.'

'Can I come too?' said Owlglass.

'See?' said Bane. 'Imagine what a difference *five* can make. And if we're wrong, it won't matter. But if we're right . . . what else can we do? Run around? Shout? Try to raise an army? Let's sort it out *now*.'

'Anyway, the palace walls are too high. And very thick,' said Pismire.

'Nothing will stop a pone going where it wants to go,' said Bane. 'Or me!'

'I always wondered,' said Brocando, in the sudden silence, 'and now I know.'

'Know what, for goodness sake?' said Pismire, thoroughly rattled.

'Why the Dumii conquered the Carpet,' said the king. 'It was because, every once in a while, they thought like this.'

After a while Glurk said, 'Anyone any idea about how we get in?'

Chapter 19

Snibril was also learning something. He was learning about the power of sergeants.

Careus had found the palace kitchens, because sergeants always know how to find a kitchen. It was a long low room, with half a dozen fireplaces and a blackened ceiling.

And then he'd found the head cook, who was an old friend.

'This is Mealey,' he said, introducing Snibril to a huge red-faced man with a scar across his nose, a patch over one eye and only one arm. 'He used to be in the army, like me.'

'Was he a sergeant too?' said Snibril.

'That's right,' said Mealy, grinning. The scar seemed to grin, too. When he stepped around the table, Snibril saw that he had a wooden leg. 'Seen action in dozens o' campaigns,' said Mealey, following his gaze. 'Then one day Careus here picked me up and carried me back to safety and said Mealy, boy, you better retire right now while there's still some of you left to send home. Good to see you again, mate.'

'Strange stuff happening, Mealy,' said the sergeant.

'No error. Top brass been sacked all over the place. No-one's seen the Emperor for a fortnight. Spends all his time in his rooms. Has all his meals sent in.'

'And these advisers,' said Snibril. 'What about them?'

'No-one's seen 'em,' said Mealy, scratching his back with a ladle. 'But I bin up there with a tray one time and they smell—'

'Moulish?' said Snibril.

Several other cooks had wandered up and were listening with interest. They all looked very similar to Mealy. There were half a dozen of them, but only enough arms and legs and ears and eyes for about four whole people. And most of them had scars that you could play noughts-and-crosses on.

'Right,' said Mealy. 'And I bin pretty close to mouls enough times to know what I'm smellin'. We don't like it. But there's only the handful of us. If we had some lads with us . . .'

Careus and Snibril looked at one another.

'They're right here, in the palace,' said Snibril.

He looked around at the cooks. They were all very big men.

'You were all sergeants, weren't you,' he said. 'I can tell.'

'Well, you see,' said Mealy, 'you learn about arranging things, when you're a sergeant. Like, you make sure that when you retires you gets a cushy number. In the warm all day. Reg'lar meals. Old sergeants get everywhere.'

'Let's go and—' Snibril began.

He stared into the darkness at the end of the sooty kitchen.

'Who's she?' he said.

'Who?'

The sergeants turned.

Snibril hesitated. 'There was someone there,' he mumbled. 'In white. And this white animal by her. And she was saying—'

He stopped.

'No women in the kitchens,' said Mealy. 'The reason being, women aren't any good at sergeanting.'

Snibril shook himself. Must have imagined it, he told himself. It's been a busy time . . .

'Sergeant Careus, can you get back and bring the army?' he said.

'To attack Ware?' said Careus.

'To defend it,' said Snibril.

'Who will we be fighting?'

'By the time you get back I hope we'll have an enemy,' said Snibril. 'Have you cooks got any weapons?'

Mealy grinned. He picked up a long meat cleaver from a big wooden table, swung it in his one arm, and brought it down on a chopping block. The chopping block split.

'Who, us?' he said.

The guards on the palace gate were nervous anyway. They didn't like their job. But orders are orders, even if you're not sure where they came from. At least, they are to a Dumii. If we didn't obey orders, where would we be?

And they were even more nervous when four heavily-cloaked wights turned up at the gate, pushing a cart. One of the guards stepped forward.

'Halt!' he said.

His companion nudged him. 'They're wights,' he said, 'I don't think you can say Halt to wights. They must have a reason to go in.'

'That's right,' said one of the wights.

The first guard said, doubtfully, 'But one of them's eating a cucumber . . .'

'I expect wights have to eat.'

'And there's only four of them. There ought to be seven,' said the first guard.

'We've been ill,' said a wight.

Another wight added, 'Although, of course, when we say *we* we don't mean—'

A wight nudged him in the ribs. The first guard was not going to give up easily.

'I don't think you're wights at all,' he said. The wight who was eating cucumber turned its hood towards him.

'Can prove it,' it said. 'Can tell you the future.'

'Oh, yes?'

The wight took a club off the cart.

'Going to get hit,' said Glurk.

'Not too hard,' said Bane, pushing his hood back. 'He's just in the way. He's not an enemy.'

Glurk hit the guard in as friendly a way as possible. The second guard started to draw his sword and opened his mouth to shout, but he felt something pointed touch his back.

'Drop the sword,' said Pismire.

'And when we say *drop*, we mean let go of in a downward direction,' said Owlglass, hopping up and down. 'Isn't this exciting!'

Mealy knocked on a large, ornate door. Two cooks behind him were pushing a trolley. It was a large one; a white tablecloth hung down on all sides.

After a while a courtier opened the door.

'Dinner,' said Mealy. 'Bring it in?'

'Oh. The cook. Very well,' said the courtier. The trolley was wheeled through. There were a couple of guards sitting on the bench in the room beyond. They didn't look very happy.

There was another door beyond. The courtier opened it.

There was yet another room beyond. It was empty. There was another closed door in the opposite wall.

'Leave it in there,' said the courtier. 'Then be off.'

'Right, right,' said Mealy. The cooks pushed the trolley into the next room. Then they filed out obediently. The courtier closed the inner door.

'Don't you ever wonder what happens next?' said Mealy.

'It's not my job to wonder about the Emperor's business,' sniffed the courtier, 'and certainly not with a *cook*.'

'In fact,' said Mealy, taking off his tall cook's hat, 'I'm a sergeant. You lads there – attention!'

The two guards stood to attention before they realized what they were doing. Several more cooks filed into the room. Each of them was carrying something sharp.

'This is—' the courtier began, and then realized that he was in a room with half a dozen large armed men, who probably were not ready to be shouted at.

'—against orders,' he said.

'We've put the food in there. That *was* orders,' said Mealy. He limped over to the door and put his one ear to it. 'We're just waiting to see what happens next.'

The long cloth made a sort of mobile tent.

He heard the door shut behind him. After a minute or two, another door opened.

He smelled moul. It was not in fact a particularly bad smell; they smelled like a fur coat that hadn't been brushed for too long.

The trolley moved. The door shut, and this time it shut *behind* him, in a very final kind of way.

The moul smell was overpowering. And only now did he hear voices.

'Your dinner, sire.' A moul voice.

'I'm not hungry!' A human voice, but with a sulky whine in it that suggested that its owner had been given too many sweets when he was young and not enough shoutings-at. It was the kind of voice that's used to having its life with the crusts cut off.

'Sire must eat,' moul voice, 'otherwise there will be nothing left of sire.'

'What's happening outside? Why won't you tell me what's happening outside? Why doesn't anyone do what I tell them?' Snibril thought he heard a foot stamp. He'd never believed that people really did that outside stories.

'The civil war rages on,' another moul voice, 'you have enemies on all sides. Only we can protect you. You must let us do that, sire.'

'Call Fray down on them!' The Emperor, thought Snibril, horrified. Only well-bred people can be as rude as that.

'Soon, soon, just as we did in Jeopard,' a third moul voice. 'In the meantime, my people are fighting hard on your behalf. Perhaps we shall have to call on Fray, in time.'

'I am surrounded by enemies!' whined the Emperor.

'Yes, yes,' said a moul voice, as if it was talking to a baby.

'And everyone must do what I say!'

'Yes, yes,' moul voice. 'Within reason.'

'You know what happens to enemies,' said the Emperor. 'They get sent away. To a bad place!'

Our village wasn't that bad, thought Snibril. Pismire used to say it was full of homely comfort. I thought the Emperor was going to be noble!

'I'm hungry now. Have you finished tasting my food?'

'Not quite, sire.'

'But it's nearly all gone!'

'Poison could be even in the last bite,' said a moul voice, and it occurred to Snibril it was speaking with its mouth full.

'Yeh. Yes, of course you're right,' said the Emperor uncertainly. 'I've never trusted those cooks. They've got far too many bits missing. Even so – perhaps a crust?'

'Why, certainly, sire. And I think we can trust a little of this gravy . . .'

We've come all the way to defend *this*? thought Snibril.

And then he thought: what would Bane say about this?

He'd say: he's the Emperor, whatever else he might be. You've got to do something.

All right, what would Pismire say? He'd say: listen and observe and then take unprecipitate action based on received information. So *that's* not much help.

Brocando would, say no, he'd *shout*: Attack!

Glurk wouldn't even wait to shout.

Oh well. I just hope Mealy is still outside.

Bane peered around a corner, and then beckoned the others.

'Don't look too conspiratorial,' said Pismire. 'If we walk as if we've got a right to be here, the guards won't take any notice.'

'I'm fed up with skulking around,' said a very small wight behind him. 'That's no way for a king to behave.'

Bane threw off his robe.

'I thought those guards took it very well, considering,' said Pismire.

'Considering what?' said Glurk.

'Considering we've just hit them. They positively wanted to be tied up, I thought. They didn't like what they had to do.'

'They still did it, though,' said Brocando. 'They still obeyed orders. Stupid. What would Deftmenes be if we went around obeying orders all the time?'

'They might be ruling the Carpet,' said Pismire.

'Ha!' said Brocando, 'but the trouble about obeying orders *is*, it becomes a habit. And then everything depends on who's giving the orders.'

They reached another archway. There were two more guards there, Glurk gripped his stick.

'No,' said Bane. 'Let's do it my way this time.'

He stepped forward.

'You men – eyes face! Preeeesent armssss! Very good. Very good. Come on, people—'

One of the soldiers looked doubtful.

'Got orders to let no-one through,' he managed.

'We're not anyone,' said Bane. 'And that's an order.'

The guard stood to attention.

'Yessir. Verygoodsir!' he said.

'Don't talk to me, I'm not here,' said Bane.

The guard started to speak, and then nodded instead.

'Good man. Come on.'

Owlglass tapped the guard on the shoulder as he passed through.

'Of course, when we say "not here" we mean only in a figurative or—'

Pismire grabbed him by his collar. 'Come on!'

There were four mouls in the room, staring at Snibril in astonishment. There was also a young man of about his age, who oddly enough was reacting faster than the mouls. By the time he spoke he'd passed right through astonishment and into anger. The Emperor raised a pudgy hand, covered in rings.

'He's not a cook!' he wailed. 'He's all there! So why's he here?'

Snibril dropped his spear and grabbed the arm. 'You come with me,' he said, and added, 'sire.' He waved his sword at the mouls. 'It's one against four,' he said. 'That means I'm four times more likely to hit one of you, and who knows which one it'll be?'

The mouls hadn't moved. Then one of them smiled. The Emperor struggled in Snibril's grip.

'Very wise, sire,' said the moul who had smiled.

'I'm here to rescue you!' said Snibril. 'These are *mouls*! They're destroying the Empire!'

'The Empire is safe and well,' said the Emperor smugly.

150

Snibril was astonished. 'What about Fray?' he said.

'Jornarileesh and his people can control Fray,' said the Emperor. 'Fray only strikes my enemies. Isn't that so?'

'Yes, sir,' said the one called Jornarileesh. He was a tall moul. This one's not like Gormaleesh, Snibril thought. This one looks clever.

'It's striking everywhere!' shouted Snibril.

'That proves I have a lot of enemies,' said the Emperor.

The mouls were advancing and, suddenly, the Deftmene way of calculating odds was beginning to seem a lot less attractive.

'Drop the sword and let go of him,' said Jornarileesh. 'If you don't, we will call down Fray.'

'Right now?' said Snibril.

'Yes!'

'Right this minute?'

'Yes!'

'Do it, then.'

'No!' wailed the Emperor.

Snibril's head felt quite clear. 'You can't,' he said. 'They can't, sire. It's just a threat. They can't do it. They're no different than me!'

Now he had time to look around he could see, in one corner of the big room, a hole. It had bits of hair around the edges.

'You came up from Underlay,' he said. 'That was clever. Dumii obey orders, so all you had to do was be in the – the centre, where they start. All you had to do was frighten this . . . this idiot!'

The Emperor went red with anger. 'I will have you exec—' he began.

'Oh, shut up,' said Snibril.

The mouls drew their swords and dashed towards him. But four on to one was a disadvantage; it meant that each one was really waiting for one of the other three to make the first move.

151

There wasn't any cutting, thrusting and parrying; that only happens when people are fencing with swords for fun. When it's for real, it's like two windmills with sharp edges. The idea is to cut the other person very badly, not to look impressive.

Snibril backed towards the door, fending off blows as best he could. One of the mouls shouted something in its own language, and another couple of heads appeared over the edge of the hole.

Snibril kicked the door. 'Mealy! Open up!'

The door swung open. The room beyond was empty. Snibril dragged the Emperor into it.

And the mouls made the mistake of chasing them. The cooks had been standing behind the doors. They stepped, or at least hopped, out.

Mealy hit a moul over the head with a ladle.

'There's seven of us and four of them,' he said. 'It's not fair. Three of us won't have anyone to hit. Get 'em, lads!'

'There's more coming out of a hole in the floor!' said Snibril, still hanging on to the Emperor.

'Good!'

'What's happening? Why is all this happening?' said the Emperor. He didn't look angry any more. He looked frightened, and a lot younger. Snibril almost felt sorry for him.

The cooks were disappointed. Most of the mouls scurried back into the Emperor's chambers, diving into the hole and colliding with one another in their desperation to escape.

Mealy's kitchen army dragged a heavy table across the room and upended it over the hole.

Mealy wiped his hand on his apron. 'There,' he said. 'All done.'

'I'm afraid we're only just beginning,' said Snibril. 'There could be thousands of them underneath us right now—'

152

'Everyone must do what I say!' screamed the Emperor. 'I am in charge!'

The sergeants turned to look at him.

'We ought to protect the Emperor,' said one of them.

'We could shove him down the hole with those friends of his,' said Mealy. 'They'd protect him all right.'

The Emperor's little piggy eyes glanced from Mealy to the table to Snibril and back again.

Then he shouted, 'Guards!'

The door to the passageway banged open, and a couple of armed men stepped into the room.

'I want these men locked up!' shouted the Emperor.

'Really?' said Bane. 'What for?'

An hour makes a lot of difference.

They brought the army in. In order to save a lot of explaining, they did it by getting a signed order from the Emperor.

It was signed of his own free will, after Glurk explained patiently that if it *wasn't* signed of his own free will, there would be trouble.

Then there was a council of war.

'I always knew this would happen,' said Bane. 'Once upon a time the Emperor was elected. Then Targon made it hereditary, so that stupid brat of his could take over. Hardly anyone objected! It's as bad as having *kings*.'

'That's going too far!' said Brocando.

'I'm sorry. You're right. At least the Deftmenes have had kings for a long time. At least you're good at being kings.'

'Don't start arguing,' said Snibril. 'We ought to be wondering what the mouls are doing.'

'They're doing what they always do,' said Bane. 'They're waiting for Fray, so they can attack when everyone is disorganized. They just got a bit impatient here.'

153

'We might be lucky,' said Owlglass. 'Of course, when I say lucky—'

'It'll happen,' said Pismire, despondently. He waved a map in front of him. 'The village and Jeopard and Ware are more or less in a straight line.'

'Does that mean anything?' said Snibril.

'Nothing good,' said Pismire. 'Where's the Emperor?'

'Glurk and the cooks have got him locked up in the kitchens,' said Bane. 'Best way. He can't eat and shout at the same time.' He looked down at a scrap of paper in front of him. 'With every fighting man we've got, we're still less that fifteen hundred people,' he said.

'Less than that, in fact,' said Pismire. 'You can't leave women and children and old people in the city. Remember Tregon Marus. Buildings fall down. We'll have to get them to safety and guard them.'

'No. Arm the women,' said Brocando.

'Don't be stupid,' said Bane. 'Women don't know how to fight.'

'Deftmene women do,' said Brocando.

'Oh, yes? Who with?'

'Deftmene men,' said Brocando.

'He's got a point,' said Pismire. 'My granny had a wallop like a wrestler. I think she could go through a moul like a hot knife through runny butter.'

'I absolutely forbid it,' said Bane. 'Women fighting? That's not warfare. That's just a vulgar mess. No. I mean it. I want that absolutely understood, Your Majesty. Get them to safety, yes – but no fancy ideas. Besides, they wouldn't have the first idea about tactics.'

'Fine,' said Brocando. 'All right. No fighting women.' Snibril noticed that he was grinning in a funny way.

'Besides,' said Bane, 'there's not enough weapons to go round as it is.'

'There's a whole armoury in the palace!' said Owlglass. 'When we unlocked it there was nothing in there but a hole in the floor,' said Bane. 'The mouls have got them.'

'Well, then—' Brocando began.

'You're going to suggest we attack the mouls to get weapons off them, aren't you,' said Bane coldly.

'Well—' Brocando began.

'Don't,' said Bane. He slapped his hand on the table. 'They're out there,' he said, 'and down there. I know it. Just waiting. After Fray strikes, they'll attack. That's how it'll happen. That's how they do it, if they can't worm their way in from inside.'

Snibril had been listening to this. When he finally spoke, he felt as though he was reading words off a page. These were the words he had to say now.

'I can help,' he said. They all looked at him.

'I can sense when Fray is coming,' he said. 'I'm not as good at it as the mouls, but I'm better than most animals.'

'It's true,' said Sergeant Careus. 'I've seen him do it.'

'Well, that'll be a help,' said Bane.

'No, you don't understand,' said Snibril. 'What do the mouls do before Fray strikes?'

'How should I know,' said Bane. 'Lie down and put their hands over their eyes, if they're sensible. And then attack immediately.'

He seemed to think about this.

'When they expect to find a crushed enemy,' he said.

Snibril nodded.

Pismire said, 'It might work, you know. Forewarned is forearmed.'

There was silence. And then Brocando said, 'Four armed? Does that mean we can hold twice as many swords?'

155

Chapter 20

They won.

And that was more or less all that the history books said, later, after New Ware was built out of the rubble of the city. They were more concerned with the election of Bane as President, since he was considered to be honest and brave and without any imagination. The Dumii distrusted imagination – they said it made people unreliable.

The people who wrote the history books weren't there. They didn't know how it *happened*.

And all the other ways it could have gone.

First, there was the question of weapons. Mealy took charge of that. Spears, for example. You tied a kitchen knife on the end of a stick and you couldn't tell the difference. Especially if it got stuck in you. And a handful of nails in a piece of hair made the kind of club that wasn't exclusive at all – you could hit *anyone* with it. The sergeants lined up every able-bodied man and boy in the city and gave them simple demonstrations.

Glurk spent a lot of time helping them. Mealy said he was one of nature's sergeants, whatever *that* meant.

Brocando was put in charge of guarding the women and children. Snibril thought he grinned too much when he agreed to this. And Bane was everywhere, giving orders. Making plans. Supervizing the special work that was hurriedly being carried on just outside the walls.

Pismire and Owlglass played a game. It consisted of moving little models of warriors around on a board made of squares. Pismire said he played because it concentrated the mind, and also because Owlglass bet heavily and wasn't very good.

Snibril felt at a loose end.

Eventually he found Bane, who was leaning on the battlements over one of the main gates, looking out at the hairs. There were always guards here, with a bugle to warn the city in case of attack.

'Can't see anything,' said Snibril. 'We've sent patrols out. They didn't find anything.'

'I wasn't looking for mouls,' said Bane.

'What were you looking for, then?'

'Hmm? Oh. No-one,' said Bane.

'A figure in white,' said Snibril. 'I've seen her, too.'

'She has to watch, to make things happen . . .' Bane seemed to pull himself together. 'I don't like this,' he said, briskly. 'It's too quiet.'

'Better than too noisy,' said Snibril.

'How's your head?'

'Can't feel anything,' said Snibril.

'Sure?'

'Feels fine.'

'Oh.'

Bane looked out at the special defences. Everyone who could be spared had worked on them, digging trenches in the dust and piling it up as a low wall. From the hairs, no-one could see anything.

'That's all Ware was, once,' he said. 'Just a ditch and a wall. And enemies all around.'

'Glurk thinks the mouls have all gone. They must have heard us. Why do they attack us anyway?'

'Everyone's got to do something,' said Bane, still gloomy.

'Look,' said Snibril, 'Everyone's ready. About as ready

as they can be, anyway. We've blocked all the holes! What's going to happen next? You've got the Emperor in prison! What's going to happen afterwards?'

'Do you think there's going to be an afterwards?' said Bane.

'There's always an afterwards,' said Snibril. 'Glurk said that's what Culaina told you. The point is to get the afterwards you want.'

He scratched his head. There was an itch behind his ear.

'There's a limit to how long we can stay ready, anyway,' said Bane.

Snibril rubbed his ear again.

'Bane—!'

'If we're ready at all. I thought from what you said that the wights might help, but they just ran off—'

'Bane—!'

Bane turned.

'Are you all right?'

Snibril felt that his ears were being pressed into the middle of his head.

'Fray?' said Bane.

Snibril nodded, and even *that* hurt.

'How long have we got?'

Snibril held out a hand, all fingers extended. Bane strode along the top of the wall to the nearest guard and picked up the bugle. Dust billowed out when he blew it.

It's a funny thing. When there's a warning signal, when people have known for *ever* that there's a warning signal, and that warning signal is sounded for the very first time . . . people don't react properly. They wander out blearily saying things like 'Someone's mucking about with the warning signal, aren't they?' and 'Who's blowing the warning signal? That's for *warnings*, that is.'

158

Which is what happened now. Bane looked down at the streets filled with bewildered people, and groaned.

'It's starting!' he shouted. 'Now!'

A Dumii raised a hand uncertainly.

'Is this another practice?' he said. There had been a lot of practices in the last few days.

'No!'

'Oh. Right.'

A moment later the air was filled with shouted orders.

Snibril sank to his knees as Ware emptied itself around him.

'. . . squad three! Main square! Keep away from buildings! . .'

'. . . bandages, bandages, who's got the bandages? . .'

'. . . remember, they can come up from underneath! . .'

All Snibril wanted to do was crawl into a hole and pull it in after him. His head felt flat.

'. . . OK, line up the pones! . .'

He could get away, anyway. Staggering, ignored by everyone else, he almost fell down the ladder from the battlements and groped his way towards the rail where he had tethered Roland. He pulled himself on to the horse's back and joined the flow of people leaving Ware.

Then the animals started to feel the effects of Fray. The pones, which were already outside the gate, started to trumpet. Horses neighed, and several bolted towards the hairs outside the city walls. Dogs and cats ran between the feet of the people.

They want to get away, Snibril thought dully.

The houses began to tremble, very gently.

Then, with no sound yet, the hairs that arched over the city began to bend.

Then came the creaking – long and drawn out, as thousands of hairs were forced downwards by the tremendous weight.

It's right overhead, Snibril thought.

159

The people leaving Ware didn't need any more encouragement. The hairs over the city were getting closer, groaning and creaking as the weight pushed them down.

We'll never do it all in time . . .

Roland cantered through the arch of the gateway.

The walls collapsed. The ground moved like the skin of an animal, smashing the houses. Ware began to fall in on itself.

Snibril's ears popped. The relief almost made him want to cry.

He looked back at the city. Walls were still toppling as the Carpet itself bent under Fray, but nearly everyone had got out.

A couple of soldiers barrelled through the archway just before it broke.

Right over us, Snibril thought. As if something wants to kill us. But Pismire thinks Fray is just some kind of natural force we can't understand. Would that be any better? Thousands of us, killed by something that *doesn't even know we are here*?

There were a few people still visible outside the city, and nothing could hide the pones.

He looked at the hairs around Ware.

Which erupted mouls. He had time to turn Roland around and race back towards the city.

Bane's head poked up as Roland leapt over the ditch in the dust.

'There's thousands of them!'

'Wait until they get closer,' said Bane.

Mouls and snargs were still pouring into the clearing.

Snibril looked along the ditch. At this point most of the defenders were Dumii bowmen, lying down calmly and watching the black wall moving towards them.

'Aren't they close enough *yet*?'

'Not yet,' said Bane. 'Sergeant Careus . . . give the signal to be ready.'

160

'Yessir!'

Snibril could make out individual creatures now.

Bane scratched his chin. 'Not yet,' he said, 'not yet. The first shot is the most . . . important.'

There was a flicker on the mound of dust behind them. Snibril and Bane turned to see a white figure, staring intently at the onrushing horde. Then it vanished.

'Sergeant Careus?' said Bane quietly.

'Sir?'

'The moment is *now*.'

Sergeant Careus threw back his shoulders and grinned.

'Yessir! Squad one . . . wait for it, wait for it . . . squaaaaad one . . . fire! Squad one back! Squad two forward! Squaaaaad two . . . fire! Squad one reload! Squad one forward! Squaaaaad one . . . fire . . .'

Not many people had even seen Dumii archers in action – or rather, they had, but since arrows had been heading towards them they'd never had much of a chance to make detailed notes. Their technique was simply to keep arrows flying towards the enemy. The bowmen didn't have to be good. They just had to be fast. It was like watching a machine at work.

There was a howl from the attackers. That was another Dumii lesson – hit the front line of a rushing attack, and the enemy had to spend too much time trying to avoid tripping over itself. Bowmen started hurrying along the ditch in both directions, leaving only a small squad to carry on the fight there.

Snibril went with them.

There had been archers all around the circle. Only in one place had the mouls been able to get right up to the ditch, and there were two fights going on – Deftmenes were fighting mouls, and other Deftmenes were fighting the first Deftmenes to get a chance to fight mouls too.

Deftmenes had a technique for fighting enemies three times as high as they were – they'd run up them until they got to shoulder height, and hang on with one hand and fight with the other. It meant that half the mouls were stabbing at their own heads.

There were two more charges before it dawned on the mouls that things had gone wrong.

They grouped around the hairs, and there were still too many of them.

'We could keep this up all day,' said Brocando.

'No we can't,' said Bane.

'We haven't lost anyone yet!'

'Yes, but do *you* want to go and ask the mouls if we can have our arrows back?' said Bane.

'Oh.'

'We've got enough for one more charge, and that's it. And if it comes to hand-to-hand fighting – they've got more hands than we have.'

'I thought we were four-armed.'

'Figure of speech. 'We're outnumbered and out-weaponed.'

'Good,' said Brocando. 'We like a challenge.'

'Here they come again,' said Snibril. 'Hang on – just a few of them. Look.'

Half a dozen snargs were trotting out of the lines. They stopped halfway between the moul army and the remains of the city.

'They want to talk,' said Bane.

'Can we trust them?' said Glurk.

'No.'

'Good. I'd hate to trust something like them.'

'But you should talk,' said Pismire. 'It's always worth talking.'

In the end they rode out to the mouls. Snibril recognized the leader, who now had a crown of salt crystals and watched them imperiously. But Bane was more interested in Gormaleesh, who was among the party.

'Well?' said Bane. 'What do you have to say?'

'My name is Jornarileesh,' said the moul with the crown. 'I offer you peace. You cannot win. Time is on our side.'

'We have plenty of weapons, and plenty of men to use them,' said Bane.

'And plenty of food?' said Jornarileesh.

Bane ignored this. 'What kind of peace do you offer?'

'Throw away your weapons,' said Jornarileesh. 'Then we will talk further.'

'Throw away my sword *first*?' said Bane, as if he was considering the question.

'Yes. You have no choice.' Jornarileesh's gaze swept from face to face. 'Not one of you. Accept my conditions, or you will die. You six will die here, and the rest of your people will die soon.'

'You can't listen to him!' said Snibril. 'What about Jeopard and the High Gate Land?'

'Throw away my sword,' said Bane, slowly. 'It's an attractive idea, though.'

He drew the sword and held it up.

'Gormaleesh?' he said.

Bane's arm moved in the blur of speed. The sword slid through the air like a knife, hitting the moul in the throat. Gormaleesh dropped silently, staring in horror.

'There,' said Bane. 'That's how we throw our swords away in Ware. I did warn him. He just wouldn't listen.'

He turned his horse and galloped back to the city, with the others trying to keep up. Jornarileesh hadn't moved a muscle.

'That was very un-Dumii of you,' said Pismire. 'I'm surprised.'

'No. Gormaleesh was surprised. You were just amazed,' said Bane. 'He was drawing his sword. Didn't you see?'

'They're getting ready for another charge,' said Glurk.

'I'm surp—amazed they haven't tried digging up from Underlay,' said Pismire.

163

'Some did,' said Glurk, with satisfaction. 'They came up under Mealy's squad. They won't try *that* again.'

Bane looked back at the worried faces of the defenders. 'Their next charge, then,' he said. 'We'll make them remember it. Get the pones ready. We'll use everything we've got.'

'Everything?' said Brocando. 'Right.' He trotted his pony back along the ditch.

They waited.

'How much food *have* we got?' said Snibril, after a while.

'Four or five meals' worth, for everyone,' said Bane, absently.

'That's not much.'

'It may be more than enough,' said Bane.

They waited some more.

'Waiting is the worst part,' said Pismire.

'No it isn't,' said Owlglass, who wasn't even being trusted to hold a sword. 'I expect that having long sharp swords stuck in you is the worst part. Waiting's just boring. When I say boring, I mean—'

'Here they come,' said Glurk, picking up his spear.

'They've moved around,' said Bane. 'Putting everything they've got on one place. Right. Has anyone got a spare sword?'

In the end, it's people fighting. Charges and counter-charges. Arrows and spears everywhere. Swords cutting bits off people. Afterwards, historians draw maps and put little coloured oblongs on them and big wide arrows to indicate that this is where the Deftmenes caught a whole crowd of mouls unawares, and *here* is where the pones trampled some snargs, and *here* is where Mealy's Irregulars were trapped and were only rescued by a determined rush by a group of Munrungs. And sometimes there are crosses – *this* is where Bane brought down a moul chief, *there* is where Owlglass laid out a snarg by accident.

The maps can't show the fear, and the noise, and the excitement. *Afterwards* it's better. Because if there's an afterwards, it's because you're still alive. Half the time no-one knows what happened until it's over. Sometimes you don't know even who's won until you've counted . . .

Snibril ducked and stabbed his way through the mêlée. There seemed to be mouls everywhere. One caught him a cut on his shoulder, and he didn't even notice until afterwards.

And then he was in a clearer area, mouls all around him, swords upraised—

'Wait.'

There was Jornarileesh, the moul leader, with a paw held up.

'Not yet. See we are not disturbed.' He looked down at Snibril. 'You were out there, with the others. And tried to save the fat little Emperor. I am curious. Why are you still fighting? Your city is destroyed. You cannot win.'

'Ware's not destroyed until we stop fighting,' said Snibril.

'Really? How can this be?'

'Because . . . because if Ware is anywhere, it's inside people,' said Snibril.

'Then we shall have to see if we can find it,' said Jornarileesh meaningfully.

There was trumpeting behind him, and the group scattered as a pone stampeded through the fight. Snibril dived for safety. When he looked back, the moul was back in the fray.

And the defenders *were* losing. You could feel it in the air. For every moul that was beaten, there were two more to take their place.

He rolled down a slope and found Bane there, holding

off a couple of the enemy. As Snibril landed, one of the mouls sunk to the ground. A backhand swipe took care of the other.

'We're losing,' said Snibril. 'We need a miracle.'

'Miracles don't win battles,' said Bane. Half a dozen more mouls appeared around the rubble of a half-destroyed building. 'Superior numbers and better tactics—'

There was a bugle call behind them. The mouls turned.

There was another army advancing. It wasn't very big, but it was determined. Brocando was in the lead. They could hear his shout over the noise.

'Madam! Hold it by the *other* end! Now, now, ladies, don't all push! Careful of that spear, you could do someone a mischief—'

'Isn't that the point, young man?' said an old lady who shouldn't have been anywhere near a battlefield.

'No, madam, *that* is the butt. The point is the sharp bit at the other end.'

'Then out of the way, young man, so's I can *use* it.'

The mouls were staring in astonishment. Snibril hit two of them over the head before the others had time to react, and by then it was too late.

The women weren't the most efficient fighters Bane had ever seen, but Brocando had spent a couple of days giving them some secret training. Mealy had helped, too. And they were keen. Besides, not having been trained as proper soldiers was even a help. Dumii soldiers learned their tic-toc sword drill, and weren't up to novel ways invented as you went along, like hitting an enemy across the back of the knees with the end of a spear and stabbing him as he fell over. The women fought *nastier*.

And it still wasn't enough.

The ring of defenders was pushed back, and back, until it was fighting in the ruins of the city itself.

And . . . was beaten. Valiantly beaten. They lost. Ware

was never rebuilt. There was never a new Republic. The survivors fled to what remained of their homes, and that was the end of the history of civilisation. For ever.

Deep in the hairs, Culaina the thunorg moved without walking. She passed through future after future, and there they were, nearly all alike.

Defeat. The end of the Empire. The end of the unim-aginative men who thought there was a better way of doing things than fighting. The death of Bane. The death of Snibril. Everyone dead. For nothing.

Now she moved without *running*, faster and faster through all the futures of Maybe. They streamed past her. These were all the futures that never got written down – the futures where people lost, worlds crumbled, where the last wild chances were not quite enough. All of them had to happen, somewhere.

But not here, she said.

And then there was one, and only one. She was amazed. Normally futures came in bundles of thousands, differing in tiny little ways. But this one was all by itself. It barely existed. It had no right to exist. It was the million-to-one chance that the defenders would win.

She was fascinated. They were strange people, the Dumii. They thought they were as level-headed as a table, as practical as a shovel – and yet, in a great big world full of chaos and darkness and things they couldn't hope to understand, they acted as though they really *believed* in their little inventions, like 'law' and 'justice'. And they didn't have enough imagination to give in.

Amazing that they should have even one chance of a future.

Culaina smiled.

And went to see what it was . . .

What you look at, you change.

*   *   *

167

The mouls pulled back again, but only to regroup. After all, there was nowhere for the Dumii to go. And Snibril thought that Jornarileesh was the sort who'd enjoy imagining them waiting for him, wondering about how it was all going to end.

He found Glurk and Bane leaning exhausted against a crumbled wall. Three Dumii women were with them; one of them was bandaging a wound on Glurk's arm with strips of what had once been a good dress.

'Well,' he said. 'At least they'll say we went down fighting – ouch . . .'

'Hold still, will you?' said the woman.

Bane said: 'I don't expect the mouls have much interest in history. After this, no more books. No more history. No more history books.'

'Somehow, that's the worst part,' said Snibril.

'Excuse me,' said one of the women, 'Er. I am Lady Cerilin Vortex. Widow of the late Major Vortex?'

'I remember him. A very honourable soldier,' said Bane.

'I'd just say that no more history books is not the worst part, young man. Dying's probably the worst part,' said Lady Vortex. 'History will look after itself.'

'I'm sure we're very . . . um . . . grateful that you have assisted,' said Bane, awkwardly.

'We haven't assisted, we've taken part,' said Lady Vortex sharply.

All around the ruins of Ware people were sitting in small groups, or tending the wounded. Two pones had been killed. They at least were easy to count. Snibril hadn't seen Brocando or Pismire for a long time.

There was movement among the enemy.

Snibril sighed. 'Here they come again,' he said, standing up.

'History, eh?' said Glurk, picking up his spear. 'One final glorious stand.'

Lady Vortex picked up a sword. She was bristling with anger. 'We shall see about *final*,' she said, in a way that made Snibril think that it would be a very unlucky moul that ever attacked her. She turned to Bane. 'And when we get out of this, young man,' she snapped, 'there's going to be some serious talking. If we're going to fight, *we're* going to have a bit of the future too—'

The mouls began to charge.

But it seemed half-hearted. The ones in the front kept on coming, but gradually the ones behind slowed down. They were shouting at one another, and looking back at the hairs. Within a few seconds, they were milling around in bewilderment.

The defenders stared.

'Why're they stopping?' said Glurk.

Snibril squinted at the shadows between the hairs.

'There's . . . something else there . . .' he said.

'More mouls?'

'Can't quite see . . . there's fighting . . . hang on . . .' He blinked. 'It's wights. Thousands and thousands of wights! They're attacking the mouls!'

Bane looked around at the defenders. 'Then we've got one choice,' he said. 'Charge!'

Caught between two armies, the mouls didn't even have a million to one chance. And the wights fought like mad things . . . worse, they fought like *sane* things, with the very best weapons they'd been able to make, cutting and cutting. Like surgeons, Pismire said later. Or people who had found out that the best kind of future is one you make yourself.

Afterwards, they found that Athan the wight had died in the fighting. But at least he hadn't known he was going to. And wights talk to each other in strange ways, across the whole of the Carpet, and his new ideas had flashed like fire from wight to wight: you don't have to accept it, you can change what's going to happen.

It was an idea that had never occurred to them before.

And *then* it was over.

No-one could find the Emperor. No-one looked very hard. No-one said anything, but somehow everyone assumed that Bane was in charge now.

It doesn't all stop with the fighting, Snibril thought. The end of the fighting is when the problems *start*, no matter if you've won or lost. There are thousands of people with one day's food and no houses, and there's still mouls out there – although I think they'll be keeping away for a while. And the Empire's in bits. And there's still the High Gate Land to deal with.

At least the question of food was easily settled. There were dead snargs everywhere. As Glurk said, there was no sense in letting them go to waste.

Bane spent all day sitting in the ruins of the palace, listening to the crowds of people who filed past him, and occasionally giving orders. A squad was sent off to Jeopard, to bring back the rest of the Munrung's carts.

Someone suggested that there ought to be a feast. Bane said, one day.

And then they brought in Jornarileesh. He'd been badly injured by a spear, but Glurk's snarg-gathering party had found him alive. They tried to drag him in front of Bane, but since he could hardly stand up there wasn't much point.

'There should be a trial,' said Pismire, 'according to ancient custom—'

'And then kill it,' said Glurk.

'No time,' said Bane. 'Jornarileesh?'

Despite his wounds, the moul raised his head proudly.

'I will show you how a moul can die,' he said.

170

'We know that already,' said Bane, matter-of-factly. 'What I want to know is . . . why? Why attack us?'

'We serve Fray! Fray hates life in the Carpet!'

'Merely a natural phenomenon,' murmured Pismire. 'Bound to yield to scientific observation and deduction.'

Jornarileesh growled at him.

'Throw him in a cell somewhere,' said Bane. 'I haven't got time to listen to him.'

'I don't think there are any cells,' said Glurk.

'Then get him to build a cell and then throw him in it.'

'But we should kill him!'

'No. You've been listening to Brocando too often,' said Bane.

Brocando bristled. 'You know what he is! Why not kill—' he began, but he was interrupted.

'Because it doesn't matter what he is. It matters what *we* are.'

They all looked around. Even Jornarileesh.

It was me, thought Snibril. I didn't realize I said it aloud. Oh, well . . .

'That's what matters,' said Snibril. 'That's why Ware was built. Because people wanted to find better ways than fighting. And stop being afraid of the future.'

'*We* never joined the Empire!' said Brocando.

'When it was time to choose, whose side were you on?' said Snibril. 'Anyway, you *were* part of the Empire. You just didn't know it. You spent so much time being proud of not being part of it that you ended up . . . well, being part of it. What would you do if the Empire didn't exist? Go back to throwing people off rocks!'

'I don't throw people off rocks!'

Jornarileesh's head turned from one to the other in fascination.

'Why did you stop?' said Snibril.

171

'Well – it just wasn't the . . . never mind!'

'These?' said Jornarileesh, in astonishment. '*These* beat me? Weak stupid people arguing all the time?'

'Amazing, isn't it,' said Bane. 'Take him away and lock him up.'

'I demand an honourable death!'

'Listen to me,' said Bane, and now the tone of his voice was like bronze. 'I killed Gormaleesh because people like that shouldn't be allowed to exist. You, I'm not sure about. But if you annoy me one more time, I'll kill you where you stand. Now . . . take him *away*.'

Jornarileesh opened his mouth, and then shut it again. Snibril stared at the pair of them. He'd do it, he thought. Here and now. Not out of cruelty or rage, but because it needed to be done.

It dawned on him that he'd much rather face a fighting-mad Brocando, or Jornarileesh in a fury, than Bane.

'Snibril's right, though,' said Pismire, as the silent moul was hurried off. 'Everyone's done things the old way. Now we'll have to find a new way. Otherwise there won't be *any* way. We don't want to have to go through all this just to start squabbling over something else. The Empire—'

'I'm not sure there's going to be an Empire again,' said Bane.

'What? But there's got to be an Empire!' said Pismire.

'There might be something better,' said Bane. 'I'm thinking about it. Lots of small countries and cities joined together could be better than one big Empire. I don't know.'

'And a voice for women,' said Lady Vortex's voice from somewhere in the crowd.

'Possibly even that,' he said. 'There should be something for everyone.'

He looked up. At the back of the group were some of the wights. They hadn't said anything. No-one knew their names.

'Something for everyone,' said Bane. 'We should talk about it—'

A wight stepped forward, and pulled back his hood, revealing that he was in fact a *her*.

'I have to speak to you,' she said.

All the wights in the room removed their hoods.

'My name is Tarillon the minemaster. We are leaving now. We think . . . we think we can feel a future now. We . . . are remembering once more.'

'I'm sorry?' said Bane.

'We have chosen a new Thread.'

'I don't understand you.'

'We are wights again. Proper wights. We think we are beginning to remember a new history so now, if you please, we will go back to our lives.' She smiled. 'I remember I said this!'

'Oh,' said Bane. He looked embarrassed, a practical man faced with something he was too busy to understand. 'Well. Good. I'm glad for you. If there's anything we can do—'

'We will meet again. We are . . . sure.'

'Well. Thank you again—'

The wights were already filing out.

Snibril slipped away after them. Behind him, he could hear people starting arguing again . . .

It was morning. The wights were hurrying away through the ruins, and he had to hurry to catch up with them.

'Tarillon?'

She turned. 'Yes?'

'Why go away? What did you mean?

She frowned. 'We tried this, this . . . deciding. We listened to Athan. He told about the way of making choices. We have tried it. It is terrible. How can you do it? Living and not knowing what will happen. Unsure at every waking morning that you will see the night. It would drive us mad! But we're wights. We can't change what we are. We've helped create a new history. Now we think we can remember it again.'

'Oh.'

'What power you must all have, to be able to face such uncertainty.'

'We think it's normal,' said Snibril.

'How strange. Strange. Such courage. Well. Goodbye. You have made up your mind to leave Ware.'

'Yes, I – how did you know that?'

She looked joyful. 'I said – we can remember things again!'

He found Roland where he had tethered him. Snibril didn't have much in his pack now. The piece of lucky dust had got lost. So had the coins. He was wearing the spare pair of boots. All he had now was a blanket, some knives, a piece of rope. A spear. You didn't really need much else.

Pismire spoke from right behind him, just as he was adjusting the saddle.

'Leaving?'

'Oh. I didn't hear you,' said Snibril.

'I've spent a lot of time with you Munrungs. You know how to creep up. And, I might add, how to creep away.'

'I'm sure people are going to sort things out,' said Snibril.

'So long as they never stop arguing,' said Pismire. 'Very important, arguing.'

Snibril turned. 'I just want to find out about the Carpet,' he said. 'What Fray is. What's at the end of it all. You said we should always ask questions . . .'

'Right. Very important, questions.'

'Do you think Bane's idea will work?'

'Who knows? It's the time to try new things.'

'Yes.' Snibril climbed into the saddle. 'Did you know the wights think we're courageous because we can make decisions? They can't do it! They can't cope with it! And we thought *they* were special. Amazing what you learn.'

'Haven't I always said so?' said Pismire.

'Well, I want to find out more! And I want to go *now*, because if I leave it, I'll never go. I want to see all the things you told me about!' Snibril said. 'The Chairleg. The Hearth. The Edge.'

'Let me know what they're like, then,' said Pismire. 'I only read about 'em.'

Snibril stopped. 'But when I was little, you told me all sorts of stories about the Carpet! You mean they weren't true?'

'Oh, they were true. Otherwise they wouldn't have been written down.' Pismire shrugged. 'Always wanted to travel, myself. Never had the time, somehow. If you can, you know, ever find the time to jot down a few notes . . .'

'Right. Hah. Yes. I will. If I find time. Well, then . . . Goodbye?'

'Goodbye.'

'And say goodbye to—'

'I will.'

'You know how it is.'

'Probably. Goodbye. Come back and tell us about it, some time.'

This last word was a shout, for Snibril had urged Roland forward. When he was no more than a speck on the road he turned and waved again.

Pismire walked slowly back to the argument.

Snibril stopped again, a little way from Ware, and breathed deeply of the Carpet air.

He felt a little sad. But there would always be somewhere to return to, somewhere. He smiled, and patted
Roland's neck. Then, with rising hope and streaming
hair, he urged the white horse into a gallop and they
disappeared among the crowding hairs.

THE END